PRAISE FOR
ORPHEUS NINE

'mysterious, comedic, terrifying, and unexpectedly moving – the rare novel that penetrates both the heart and mind at the same time . . . absolutely unforgettable'
– **Elizabeth Gilbert**

'A devastating page turner. Chris Flynn is the fifth horseman of the apocalypse. He'll decimate us with his words and we'll thank him for it.' – **Siang Lu**

CHRIS FLYNN
ORPHEUS NINE

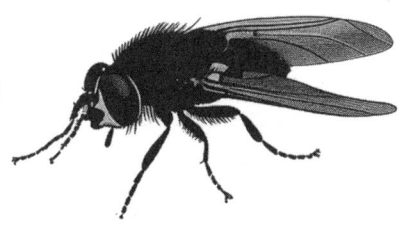

hachette
AUSTRALIA

Published in Australia and New Zealand in 2025
by Hachette Australia
(an imprint of Hachette Australia Pty Limited)
Gadigal Country, Level 17, 207 Kent Street, Sydney, NSW 2000
www.hachette.com.au

Hachette Australia acknowledges and pays our respects to the past, present and future Traditional Owners and Custodians of Country throughout Australia and recognises the continuation of cultural, spiritual and educational practices of Aboriginal and Torres Strait Islander peoples. Our head office is located on the lands of the Gadigal people of the Eora Nation.

Copyright © Chris Flynn 2025

This book is copyright. Apart from any fair dealing for the purposes of private study, research, criticism or review permitted under the *Copyright Act 1968*, no part may be stored or reproduced by any process without prior written permission. Enquiries should be made to the publisher.

 A catalogue record for this book is available from the National Library of Australia

ISBN: 978 0 7336 5227 1 (paperback)

Cover design and illustration by Alex Ross
Author photograph courtesy of Jo Duck
Typeset in 12.5/20 pt Adobe Garamond Pro by Bookhouse, Sydney
Printed and bound in Australia by McPherson's Printing Group

 The paper this book is printed on is certified against the Forest Stewardship Council® Standards. McPherson's Printing Group holds FSC® chain of custody certification SA-COC-005379. FSC® promotes environmentally responsible, socially beneficial and economically viable management of the world's forests.

As Flies to Wanton Boys   1

Part One: 9
The Orphean

Part Two: 39
The Saltless

Part Three: 71
The Decadian

Part Four: 95
The Youthful Courtesan

Part Five: 119
The Young Apostate

Part Six: 151
Heir to the Throne

Part Seven: 177
Kingdom of Hades

Part Eight: 211
Peppr

Part Nine: 249
Don't Look Back

The Cycle of Nine   281

Zubeneschamali   287

AS FLIES TO WANTON BOYS

IT BEGAN IN EVERY TOWN AND CITY AT THE SAME TIME, IN EVERY dark and twisted corner of our world. One third of the earth's citizens were asleep at the time. Their awakening was marked by horror and confusion. Just about everyone else had their routine skulking and petty games interrupted as they witnessed the event eyes wide open. They prayed it was a dream.

In the small, sleepy town of Gattan, population 7448, where everyone knew each other, sometimes a little too well, it happened at eleven o'clock on a Saturday morning. Parents and grandparents lined the oval as their beloved children and grandchildren ran and kicked and elbowed their way through organised sports like obedient automatons.

Sky van der Saar should not have been present for the soccer game, but her father insisted she attend in support of her younger brother Alex. The waste of a Saturday morning irked Sky. As a weary seventeen-year-old, there were a thousand things she'd rather have been doing, although sadly for her, none were remotely possible in Gattan. As it turned out, Sky was guiltily glad to have witnessed one of history's pivotal moments, cynical puppy that she was. She got to see the carnage firsthand.

As was often the case with such family-oriented gladiatorial contests, certain so-called adults were more vocal than others.

'Are you fucking blind, ref?' Steve Ward shouted, drawing glares from the other parents. While a no-swearing rule was in effect at the oval, for fear of offending sensitive juniors, there was little point to it. The children heard, and said, much worse at school, their words delivered with equal venom.

'Watch your language, Steve,' Sky's dad, Dirk, reprimanded him.

Steve's wife responded with her trademark stink eye. Sky's mother fixed Jess with her own look of displeasure in response. This was not easy for Lucy van der Saar, who wanted for nothing in this world – in stark contrast to Jess Ward, who had nothing.

Sky observed the tension, years of history hanging heavy between the two women. Sky was only privy to a few juicy fragments, but that was enough. She was annoyed at her mother, in any case. Lucy had made no attempt to muffle her cries of ecstasy the previous night, to Sky's disgust – her bedroom adjoined that of her parents. Sky owned the best noise-cancelling headphones money could buy, but some nights even those weren't enough.

'Come on, Tyler!' Hayley Carlisle shouted encouragement for Jess and Steve's son, but her words fell on deaf ears.

'When can I play, Mum?' Hayley's daughter asked.

'In a few months, Eb,' Hayley told her. 'You have to be nine to be on the team.'

'But Alex is on the team, and he's ten,' Ebony protested. 'He's too old now.'

Ebony had attended Alex's birthday party the previous week.

'You can take his place soon,' Lucy told her. She turned to Hayley. 'He's losing interest in sports, anyway. Head stuck in a screen all day.'

'Same as all of them,' Hayley replied.

'Not my boy,' Steve said, puffing out his chest in a misguided display of patriarchal pride. 'Get stuck into them, son!' he shouted at Tyler, who paused to acknowledge his father. 'Watch the runner on the left,' Steve added, cheeks flushed. Steve Ward was the kind of father who would never let up, his fantasy of sporting glory lived out through his son.

'We have a coach, you know,' Dirk said, indicating the beleaguered man clad in a blue Adidas tracksuit and shouting useless advice from the halfway line.

'That old fart doesn't have a clue,' Steve scoffed.

'So put your hand up to do it, then,' Dirk suggested.

'Steve's busy with work.' Jess jumped to his defence.

'Is that right?' Dirk said. 'Spike in ride-on mower sales lately?'

'As a matter of fact, yes,' Steve said, his cheeks reddening. 'And quad bikes. I sold three this week.'

'With all that commission, you'll have a deposit for your own place soon,' Dirk said, never missing an opportunity to put someone down.

Steve clenched his fists and Jess placed a placatory hand on his shoulder. *Don't take the bait.* The Wards rented, placing them amongst a minority of Gattan residents, along with the meth heads and deros.

'Where's Jude today?' Lucy asked Hayley, changing the subject.

'Went up to the city for work yesterday,' Hayley replied. 'She stayed over.'

'Not with her mum?' Lucy asked.

'God, no,' Hayley said. 'They're still not speaking. At a hotel. It was too late to drive back, what with those feral deer on the highway.'

After the last pandemic, a local venison farmer went bust. Rather than shoot the majestic animals, he opened the gate and freed them. His property adjoined one of the major country highways and there had been a dozen crashes since, three of them involving human fatalities. Now, it was stags everyone feared on the road, rather than kangaroos.

'When are those two going to bury the hatchet?' Dirk asked.

'It's a stand-off for the ages,' Hayley said, shaking her head sadly. 'They're both so stubborn. Neither one wants to back down.'

'Meanwhile, poor Ebony doesn't get to see her grandma,' Lucy said, ruffling Ebony's curly locks. Ebony jerked away from Lucy's probing fingers. She did not like people touching her hair. Maddeningly, no adult seemed able to resist.

'Who says I want to?' Ebony said. 'Mum says she's a mean old cow.'

Ebony was referring to her other mother, Jude Tan.

'You let her talk about her grandmother like that?' Lucy asked Hayley.

Hayley shrugged. 'She's not wrong.'

While they were busy talking, Tyler and Alex combined to break up an opposition play and launch a counterattack for the home team. They surged forward, passing the ball to one another, and their respective fathers began screaming encouragement from the sidelines. For a moment, even Sky was caught up in the game. That's how bored she was.

A cheer rose from the Gattan supporters. Tyler had scored a goal. He and Alex embraced as they ran back for the kick-off, while their parents leapt in the air as if they had won Tattslotto. Old animosities were temporarily forgotten. There were hugs all round.

Tyler Ward never made it back to the centre circle. He stopped abruptly and stood bolt upright, arms held tightly by his sides, his face frozen.

Alex van der Saar walked back to ask his friend what was wrong.

But he soon noticed the other nine players in his team were also immobile, as were all the opposition players. Only Alex was able to move freely. He looked to the sideline for guidance; he had no idea what was happening.

'What are they doing?' Steve asked.

The same question was on everyone's lips. The nine-year-olds on the pitch were all stuck. It was as if some god's finger had pressed the pause button on their universal remote. Tyler was close enough to the onlookers that they could see his lower lip quivering. He was trying to speak, but could not. With enormous effort, the boy managed to shift his gaze a few millimetres sideways. The fear in his eyes was plain.

Then, the children on the oval began to sing, their voices high and sweet and lovely.

Lascivi pueri ad muscas deis sumus
Nos ad ludibrium necant

'What is this, a joke?' Dirk said. 'Alex, what's going on out there?' he shouted at his son, who was the only one not singing.

'Dunno,' Alex called back. 'They never told me anything.' Alex was miffed that he had been left out of the prank.

'It's some kind of flash mob,' Hayley said, opening the camera on her phone and recording. The footage would be played on the news later that night.

'No one does those anymore,' Sky said.

'A TikTok thing, then,' Lucy suggested.

'Quit it, Tyler,' Jess Ward shouted at her son. 'Look at me.'

Tyler convulsed with effort as he struggled to turn his body towards his parents.

'Tyler?' Jess said, softening her tone as it dawned on her – as it dawned on everyone – that something was very wrong indeed.

The children sang the verse one more time.

Lascivi pueri ad muscas deis sumus
Nos ad ludibrium necant

And then the nine-year-olds fell quiet. A lull echoed across the playing field. Across the world. The adults turned to each other with quizzical, confused expressions. Only scholars of Latin would know the meaning of those words, and none present were scholars of Latin. It was a quotation from *King Lear*, one that by the end of day would be familiar to billions of people.

As flies to wanton boys are we to the gods;
They kill us for their sport.

Jess Ward's tremulous voice broke the silence.

'Ty?'

Each of the children reacted slightly differently to the sudden, massive increase of sodium in their systems, but in every recorded case around the globe the results were identical. Their hands, feet and neck became swollen beyond all normal proportions, followed immediately by kidney failure and heart attack. Within sixty seconds, every nine-year-old on the planet was dead, and the screams of brothers, sisters and parents echoed across the world.

In Gattan, only Alex van der Saar, aged ten years and one week, remained standing on the football field. He hugged himself in terror as, all around him, his friends, distended, bloated, unrecognisable, writhed in agony on the grass, and then died.

PART ONE

THE ORPHEAN

JESSICA WAS SURPRISED WHEN LUCY TEXTED TO BOOK AN in-home hairdressing appointment. Lucy usually attended the salon in town, Headlines, formerly Lunatic Fringe, formerly A Breath of FresHair. The stylists employed at Headlines were fine, but they could not provide the level of personal service Jess offered in the comfort of a client's own home. Business had boomed of late, an uptick Jess attributed to people feeling sorry for the grieving mother and wanting to funnel some cash her way. Jess was no idiot. She could see the sorrow in their eyes, and she was hardly in a position to turn down the business. Her husband had been on semi-permanent leave from his job at

Gattan Power Equipment since Tyler died. Jess was concerned he might lose the job altogether.

Steve's boss was a rule-abiding do-gooder who believed workplaces should be run like the military. Darren had established a clear chain of command, appointing himself as the no-nonsense Sergeant Major. Under Darren's rule, anyone who felt sick or depressed should suck it up and come to work anyway, rather than let the team down. He exhibited a startling lack of empathy for any parent who suffered a loss during the ongoing crisis, and he did not understand why Steve was struggling to get over the death of his son. Darren was one of those people who, having been personally unaffected by the tragedy, yearned for a return to the way things were before; he wanted everyone to move on because it was inconvenient for him. Jess found this attitude incredibly frustrating, almost as grating as those who were overly sympathetic.

Whatever the reason for the summons from Lucy, Jess didn't care. She liked to imagine Dirk had cajoled his wife into sending the text. Despite his many faults, Dirk had at least expressed genuine sorrow at Tyler's funeral. Perhaps even shed a tear, if only in Jess's imagination. Meanwhile, Steve had stood by the grave stony-faced and swaying, four Jack and Cokes deep, seconds away from falling in the hole himself.

Jess would gladly drive over to the Van der Saar mansion and run her fingers through Lucy's hair if only to see how the other half lived. When Lucy wasn't looking, she could steal an expensive trinket, or 'accidentally' smash something valuable. The Van der Saars could afford to replace crystal decanters and antique lamps. Dirk's family had owned VDS Jewellery and Watches for over a hundred years. Gattan was an early outpost for Dutch settlers, and the Van der Saars lived on Jongebloed Lane, in the big house at the top of the hill. The Paris end of town. Jess and Steve lived on the south side, next to the tip.

Jess parked her clapped-out LandCruiser behind Hairhouse Warehouse and ran in to grab a bottle of mousse. As she scanned the aisles, all eyes fell upon her. She could practically hear the whispers.

She's one of those. An Orphean. She lost her boy. Poor thing.

Jess located the mousse as quickly as she could, but she was not getting out of Hairhouse Warehouse that easily. Mrs Rayner made a beeline for her, unsteady on those elderly pins. Her mobility scooter was parked outside. The shopping plaza needed a separate parking area for such vehicles.

'I was so sorry to hear about your son,' Mrs Rayner said, cornering Jess in the hairspray section. 'It must be devastating to lose a child so young.'

'I didn't lose him,' Jess replied. 'He was taken away from me.'

'Oh, I know, it's so traumatic for everyone.' Mrs Rayner touched Jess's forearm, sending a jolt of electricity through her shoulder. 'I remember when I lost my little dog. He was such a good companion. I cried for weeks after.'

Jess was tired of the trauma vampires. They weren't sorry for her, not really. They just wanted to be involved somehow – it was almost as if they wished O9 had happened to them. So they talked about their own grief, as if it could compare. But Mrs Rayner had picked the wrong Orphean to embrace.

'You have no idea what it's like,' she said, grabbing Mrs Rayner by the hand and leaning close. 'I don't want to hear about the tragedy of little Cocoa Puff the Pomeranian and his futile yet brave battle with encephalitis. Don't you get it? My son is gone. It's not about *you*.'

The flustered Mrs Rayner tugged her hand away and withdrew.

'Only trying to offer my condolences,' she said.

'No, you're not,' Jess told her. 'You're just like all the others – the doctors, the scientists, the politicians. You don't have the slightest clue. All you can offer are platitudes. I don't need them, Mrs Rayner. Just piss off.'

The other customers remained silent until Jess paid for the mousse and exited the store. She knew they were shaking their heads behind her back, alternating between disgust and pity. Jess clambered into the LandCruiser and rested her forehead on the steering wheel, catching her breath.

One hundred and thirty million dead that first day. Three hundred and fifty thousand more every day since, each struck down at midnight GMT, the moment of their ninth birthday. For months now. And still no solutions. It wasn't a virus, it wasn't a fungal infection, it wasn't a biological terrorist attack, it wasn't an M. Night Shyamalan movie, and there was still no way to prevent kids from filling up with sodium and dying horribly in front of their distraught parents. Every eight-year-old was now a ticking time bomb. This was Orpheus Nine.

Eighty-two children had died in Gattan, including Tyler. And still no help was forthcoming. Another kid burst every couple of days.

Jess couldn't afford to keep thinking about it, and yet that day dominated her thoughts. She shook her head, took a deep breath and started the engine. Roaring out of the car park, she headed for the north side of town. She parked the LandCruiser in the driveway behind Lucy's Tesla. Of course they had an EV. Jess kicked a tyre as she walked past. Should have done their research, she thought. Jess had read an article that said lithium mining was more environmentally damaging than drilling for oil and natural gas. EVs were a con, as far as Jess was concerned, but greenies like Lucy van der Saar were so sanctimonious they couldn't face the truth, or admit when they might be wrong about anything.

'Come in, come in,' Lucy said, meeting Jess barefoot at the door. She was wearing an earth-mother kaftan made from recycled bamboo. Jess could see right through it.

'Love what you're wearing, babe,' she said to Lucy, who was oblivious to sarcasm.

Lucy raised her arms and twirled.

'Isn't it gorge?' she said. 'They're made from eco-friendly sustainable materials in an Indigenous women's commune on the north coast.'

'Sounds about right,' Jess said, patting the rear of her pants. 'I bought these on special four years ago from Just Jeans. Three pairs for seventy-five bucks. Still going strong.'

Lucy's face contorted in a patronising grimace. 'They're probably made by exploited children in India,' she said.

'At least they have children,' Jess shot back.

Lucy's expression turned grim. She gulped, unsure what to say. Jess decided to let her off the hook. Lucy was paying her, after all, and Jess was charging her more than any of her other regulars. She might even be able to buy herself a fresh pair of jeans with her new-found riches.

'Shoes off?' she asked.

'Yes, please,' Lucy said, visibly grossed out by Jess's Kmart sneakers, which had a distinctive odour only her pitbull Baz Luhrmann seemed to enjoy. The dog was forever rolling around on Jess's sneakers, and since catching Baz trying to hump one of them, she'd resorted to keeping them in a high cupboard, safely out of reach.

'Sky and Alex at school?' Jess asked as she padded through to the lounge room.

Lucy nodded. 'You want a coffee?' she asked.

'Sure,' Jess said, trying not to gawp at the lavishly decorated home. The lounge boasted high ceilings and a sunken living area. The furniture was mid-century, and the walls were adorned with contemporary art. It looked like a maniac had been let loose with a box of crayons.

'We only have French press,' Lucy said, busying herself in the vast kitchen. 'We had pods, but I got rid of them.'

'We drink instant,' Jess muttered, examining a piece of African sculpture that was begging to be called out for cultural appropriation. But Lucy had probably purchased it directly from the artist and overpaid to such an extent that his kids were now able to attend university.

'Almond milk all right?' Lucy asked.

Gotcha, Jess thought.

'Oh, I don't drink that,' she said. 'It's terrible for the environment.'

Lucy's manicured brows dipped. *Oh my Lord, she doesn't know,* Jess thought. *This is the greatest moment of my life.*

'Producing a single cup of almond milk requires almost eight litres of water,' Jess parroted the article she had read, 'and releases nearly two kilograms of carbon dioxide into the atmosphere. You can't drink that, Luce.'

Lucy's jaw dropped. She stared at the carton of almond milk like it was radioactive waste.

'Oh my God,' she said. 'I had no idea!'

Without a moment's hesitation, Lucy poured the milk down the plughole and threw the empty carton in the recycling bin.

Black coffee it is, then, Jess thought. *Oh well.*

They sat on a couch that looked fabulous but was extremely uncomfortable. Lucy folded her legs up underneath her, treating Jess to an unflattering glimpse of undercarriage that she would rather not have witnessed. Jess sipped her coffee, which she was sure had been ground from organic, free trade, ethically sourced beans that had passed through the digestive tract of a palm civet but still somehow didn't taste as nice as Moccona.

Lucy's tone turned grave, sincere. 'So, how *are* you?'

Full to the brim with grief, thanks for asking. Fucked up beyond imagining. Jess couldn't even find the energy to crawl out of bed some mornings. A dark hole had practically opened in the ground, swallowed her son and proceeded to consume everything else in his life, including her. She felt like one of those witches in medieval Europe, as if the townspeople had tied her down and placed stones on her chest, adding more and more each day until finally she was crushed under the weight of them. Steve was drinking too much and would likely get fired soon, and they were the brokest, saddest characters in that shithole trap of a town. Plus, Jess's back was sore and she had toenail rot and

Lucy was wearing a piece of diaphanous material that cost more than the LandCruiser and the coffee was fucking disgusting and she was going to pour it into one of the pot plants the minute Lucy's back was turned . . .

'Fine,' Jess said. 'Coping. What can you do? When you're going through hell . . .'

'Keep going,' Lucy said, bringing her palms together in a prayer gesture. 'That's inspiring, Jess. I'm going to include that in my affirmations.'

Great idea, Jess thought. That's what everyone said about her, of course. *You seen that Jessica Ward in her dowdy jeans and Target hoodie? What an inspirational figure.*

A tiny voice, so deep inside she could barely hear it, said something as Lucy clasped Jess's hands in hers.

Kill her, it said. *Just fucking kill her. Stab her in the toned Pilates belly with one of her three-hundred-dollar Japanese knives. You can blame it on an intruder, a drifter, a DHL delivery guy driven wild with lust when she answered the door in that transparent shift.*

'Shall we get started?' Lucy said. The formalities of grief acknowledgment and performative caring were over. It was time to get down to business – for Jess to ditch the dark fantasy and embrace her role as the hired help, come to untangle the locks of the lady of the manor. Yes ma'am, no ma'am, three bags full ma'am.

Lucy had set up a chair on the deck, next to a lap pool that belonged on the set of *The House of Gucci*. It was one of only a few pools in Gattan outside of the aquatic centre. She had also put down newspapers to protect the polished boards.

'You can wash my hair out here,' Lucy said. A bucket awaited. Metal, not plastic. Jess filled the bucket with warm water from the tap while Lucy took her place on the chair, head tipped back as if posing for an erotic photograph. Jess glanced at the sheets from *The Sentinel* spread beneath the chair. The headline chilled her. A tally of the previous day's dead, splashed across the page in bold font. The number was unimaginable. How could Lucy be so insensitive, so oblivious? Jess averted her eyes, only to spot an ad for low sodium products in one of the free supermarket supplements. They couldn't wait to get in on the act and profit from everyone's misery.

Jess focused on washing Lucy's hair with care and precision, nimble fingers massaging the woman's head as she shampooed her mane. Sometimes she wished she was a concreter instead. That way she wouldn't have to pretend to be interested in everyone. The worst part of the procedure lay in the obligation to ask how Alex was doing.

'It's hard for him,' Lucy said. 'He lost so many friends. It's been very isolating, but he's talking to someone.'

He fucking survived, what does he have to complain about? Jess thought. He should be whooping and punching the air, not wallowing in misery. Now he had an excuse to get out of everything. I can't play soccer today, sir, I've got a dose of the feels. Sad face emoji. That's all right, Alex, take your time. There'll be a place for you in the team once you're emotionally ready to rejoin the group. It was hard for Jess not to resent Lucy's son. He had lived, while hers had not, for reasons no one had been able to explain.

Desperate to change the subject, Jess inquired about Sky. She didn't know much about Lucy's seventeen-year-old daughter, but she had spotted her, late one night, tagging the abandoned service station in the company of some reprobates Lucy would definitely not approve of. That reminded her of the girl she used to be.

'She's graduating this year,' Lucy said. 'You must come to the party. It'll be good for the community to have something positive to celebrate.'

'Sure,' Jess said, but she was numb from neck to toe. She didn't care about high school graduations. Tyler would never know how that felt. In truth, Jess didn't want anything to do with children anymore. Her boy was dead, all that was finished for her now. No more Wiggles or Marvel. No whining for chocolate at the supermarket check-out. No nappies or stumbling around like a zombie, delirious with lack of sleep. No more drop-offs and pick-ups. No screaming matches because she'd bought the wrong flavour of two-minute noodles. No more Tyler. She was free. Her days were her own. And she was absolutely fucking heartbroken.

Lucy didn't notice Jess's tears because she was too rapt in the fingers deftly working shampoo through her hair. Jess had learnt how to deal with their sudden onset by now. Tears came when they wanted. She didn't fight them. She didn't blubber or wail or embarrass herself. She simply let them flow. She didn't even bother wiping her face, but let them dry and stain her cheeks. She wanted everyone to know she had been crying. Most people noticed then looked sharply away.

Oh, right. She's one of those. An Orphean. Best to say nothing. Leave her be. No reasoning with those poor women anyway. They are shells, riddled with fracture lines. Touch them and they crumble.

And then, as Jessica gazed down at Lucy van der Saar's exposed, slender neck, she heard the voice again. It wanted her to balance the cosmic scale.

Stab her in the neck with your scissors and watch her bleed out on the deck. That way she will know your pain.

Jess hefted the gleaming metal scissors, so shiny and seductive against Lucy's pale skin. For a moment, she was tempted.

* * *

A SPECIAL SECTION OF GATTAN CEMETERY HAD BEEN SET ASIDE for the children claimed by Orpheus Nine. This was echoed in cemeteries around the world. In major population centres, the sheer volume of dead posed unprecedented logistical issues that proved virtually insurmountable. New areas of land were allocated for burying children, but talk of communal graves by insensitive policymakers was quickly dismissed. Besides, the crisis was ongoing. More perished every day. Despite the mass outpouring of grief, practicality won through. These hastily created cemeteries were called Nineyards.

Gattan's Nineyard was located less than a kilometre from Jess and Steve's home, on hastily reclaimed bushland near the dump. While Steve drowned himself in drink, Jess frequently found herself at the cemetery, no matter the weather conditions. She sought a macabre solace in the rows of new gravestones, a feeling of belonging to something greater. It was also the best place to meet other Orpheans, the bittersweet name that had been bestowed upon parents who'd lost a child. Each time Jess visited the Nineyard, she experienced a sense of genuine community that was absent from all other aspects of her life. These were her people. They understood what she was going through. They were not allies perversely desperate to claim a slice of trauma for themselves, nor were they apathetic, blithely pretending everything was going to be fine. Orpheans were victims. Their suffering was real and ever-present, and their numbers swelled a little more with each passing week.

As emotional turmoil surged, so did conflicting online opinion and hysteria-laced media. This, alongside the complete failure of the world's governmental and medical agencies to propose anything close to a solution, led to a breakdown of systems, the marginalisation of ordinary citizens and the radicalisation of unsatisfied victims. As a group of people unexpectedly united by tragedy, Orpheans proved prime candidates as evangelists of conspiracy theories and rebellion.

Jess Ward was sitting by her son's grave eating a cheese and Vegemite sandwich in tribute to her boy when three other women emerged from the mist, two of them with dogs in tow. Jess called Baz Luhrmann to heel and clipped him to his leash. He loved other dogs, but pitties sometimes intimidated dog owners, who believed the hype about their unbridled savagery. But Baz didn't have a mean bone in his body. He missed Tyler terribly; Jess often found him sleeping on her son's bed. She'd packed most of Tyler's things away and stored them in the crawl space, but his presence could still be felt, and not just by her sensitive pitbull.

'Sun should burn this fog off soon,' one of the newcomers said.

'Yeah, I don't mind it,' Jess said. 'Appropriately ominous.'

The woman smiled and removed a woollen mitten to offer her hand.

'Georgia Slater,' she said. 'My daughter was Pippa. First wave.'

The dachshund at her heel sniffed Baz Luhrmann, not in the slightest bit intimidated by the size difference. Both dogs' tails wagged excitedly. Baz pawed the damp earth, whining as he tried to initiate play.

'I've seen you around,' Jess said. 'Jess Ward.' She patted the headstone. 'This is my boy Tyler, and that's Baz Luhrmann.'

Georgia laughed.

'This is Schnitzel.' She introduced her dog. 'My Pippa's three plots over.'

By mutual consent, Jess and Georgia released their dogs, who happily scampered away across the cemetery. Jess hoped Baz Luhrmann would resist the urge to dig.

The other two women gravitated to their respective children's graves, which were far enough away to be out of earshot.

'You seen the news this morning?' Georgia asked as she knelt by her daughter's headstone to tidy the flower arrangement.

'I stopped watching a while ago,' Jess said.

'I'm trying to quit, but I can't seem to stop doomscrolling,' Georgia said.

'What happened?' Jess asked.

'Huge riot in Karachi, Pakistan,' Georgia told her. 'Group of Orpheans fifty thousand strong stormed the parliament building and seized control. Army refused to fire upon them. There's talk of a coup, but it's got everyone riled up. Pakistan is a nuclear power.'

Jess snorted. 'Are the United Nations worried what a bunch of distraught mourners might do with thermonuclear warheads? They should be.'

'Bloody oath,' Georgia said. 'They're threatening to declare war on the Poms.'

'That theory's bogus,' Jess said. 'It wasn't the Brits.'

'I don't know, mate,' Georgia said. 'There's compelling evidence to the contrary. The first wave happened at midnight, Greenwich Mean Time – so, eleven o'clock in the morning here.'

'Yeah, I was there,' Jess said, irritated.

'I heard the UK government were developing a biological weapon that could be programmed to target the genomes of specific age groups,' Georgia said. 'They were going to use it to eliminate entire swathes of the population.'

'Like who?' Jess asked.

'I don't know.' Georgia shrugged. 'The poor, complainers, black people, Labour voters – whoever they think stands in the way of their insatiable lust for power.'

'And what, this bioweapon escaped from the lab somehow and decided to target nine-year-olds? Sounds dubious to me.'

'Fair point,' Georgia conceded.

'From what I've heard, London is so fucked, they'd be doing them a favour by nuking it,' Jess said, sniffing. 'Never been, myself.'

Georgia nodded and sat down on her daughter's grave, leaning back against the headstone. The woman looked bone tired, Jess thought, before realising she probably looked just as weary. Resigned to an uncertain future that would probably end with a missile exploding over the city and ending their problems in a wall of nuclear flame. The world was teetering on the brink of collapse, and the people who were supposed to be in charge were only making matters worse with their in-fighting and posturing and empty promises.

'What'd you make of the singing?' Georgia asked, lighting a roll-up cigarette that smelled like homegrown bud.

'Well, Tyler couldn't speak Latin, so fucked if I know,' Jess said.

'Pippa was in the shower when it happened,' Georgia said. 'Figured it was just nonsense lyrics she'd heard on TikTok. Had to break the door down to get to her. I was too late, obviously.'

'You couldn't have saved her,' Jess said. 'Consider yourself fortunate you didn't see it happen.'

Georgia scowled and squinted against the smoke.

'Nothing fortunate about it,' she said.

'At least we weren't locked down this time,' Jess offered.

'Yeah, fuck that,' Georgia said. 'They could never have enforced it. Too much erosion of trust after the Covid debacle. You get vaxxed?'

'Of course I did,' Jess said. 'I'm a hairdresser. It was the only way I could work.'

'More fool you,' Georgia said. 'I downloaded a fake certificate.'

'Did you catch it?' Jess asked.

'Shit, yeah,' Georgia told her. 'Omicron. I was sick as a dog. You?'

Jess shook her head. 'Not even a sniffle,' she said.

'Bit different this time, eh?' Georgia drew deeply on the joint before offering it to Jess, who politely declined.

'I'm paranoid enough,' she said.

Georgia was right. This emergency was unlike any of the others that had slammed humanity in recent years. There was no vaccine. No restrictions on societal movement. No plan to arrest the melting permafrost. No demagogue to save the day. Not even any monetary assistance. Western nations were already in recession or on the brink of financial meltdown. The advent of Orpheus Nine had plenty of people feeling like humanity was trapped inside a coffin, and that each crisis was just another nail in the lid.

'It's the end of days,' Georgia said, stubbing out the joint on her daughter's gravestone, a gesture that Jess found disrespectful.

'Maybe,' Jess said. 'At least we're still here.'

'Not all of us,' Georgia said. 'You hear about Melanie Whalen? You know Mel? Worked at Bakers Delight in the plaza.'

'Short bob with red tips?' Jess said. 'Not really, but yeah, she was in the year below me at school.'

'Necked herself,' Georgia said, making an obscene choking gesture with her tongue lolling.

'Fuck,' Jess said. 'Are you serious?'

'It's not uncommon,' Georgia said. 'Considered it myself, truth be told.'

Their conversation was interrupted by frenzied barking coming from the far side of the cemetery.

'Schnitzel, get back here!' Georgia bellowed, scaring Jess with her abrupt volume. The dachshund came loping out of the mist, Baz Luhrmann trailing behind. The pittie sprinted back to Jess and leapt onto her lap, rolling over for attention. His muddy paws stained her jeans, but Jess didn't mind. Her dog's unquestioning devotion was something upon which she had come to depend.

'We'd better shoot off before Schnitzel causes a ruckus,' Georgia said, getting to her feet and clipping the leash back onto her dog's collar. She took a treat from her pocket and handed it to the dachshund, who gobbled it greedily. Jess stood up to say goodbye and, to her surprise, Georgia embraced her, holding on a little too long.

'We need to stick together,' she said. 'You been on the forums?'

Jess shook her head. 'Nah, I've been staying offline,' she said. 'It's too overwhelming.'

'OrpheanMoms is the best one,' Georgia said. 'Check it out. Give me your number and I'll send you some links.'

Jess thanked her and they exchanged numbers, then Georgia Slater and Schnitzel the dachshund walked away across the Nineyard, mist dissipating as the morning sun warmed the damp earth. Jess watched them go until she was distracted by the sound of Baz Luhrmann pissing on his young master's gravestone, back leg cocked guiltily in the air.

***

THE GATTAN PUBLIC LIBRARY MAY NOT HAVE BEEN MUCH, BUT IT had always been a refuge for lost souls. Hidden away in the arcade connecting Murray and Graham streets, the modest amenity shared a dimly lit corridor with Sparkle & Shine nail and foot spa, the One Stop Diskount Shop, Dollar Curtains and Blinds and, at the point where the arcade emerged onto Graham Street, the Gattan Souvlaki & Chicken Hub. Walking through the arcade was an assault on the olfactory senses, the smell of cooking lamb mingling with acetone unpleasantly.

Anyone seeking refuge from the noxious fumes encountered another odour upon entering the bookish haven. Even before the housing crisis, Gattan had its fair share of swagmen living in the local bushland. Now, homeless numbers had increased dramatically, and the library represented one of the few warm, welcoming places in town. There was free instant coffee and wi-fi. Soft chairs where you could take a nap. Public computers. All the books and magazines a person could ever desire.

Jess had been a member of the library since she was a child. She sometimes felt she'd learnt more from the library than she ever had at school. As she walked through the alarm gate, she pinched her nose. There were half-a-dozen wraiths perched on stools by the window, sipping coffee from Styrofoam cups. Some stared out the window, perhaps contemplating their fate or wondering where they would sleep that night. Others were head down in books. The stink of urine and sweat that rose off these forgotten people hovered in a purple cloud by the library entrance.

Jess moved past them quickly, venturing deeper into the library, in search of a free PC she could use. They were all occupied, but the librarian assured her that one would soon become available. She perused the DVD box sets to kill time. She and Steve had recently unsubscribed from all their streaming services. Money was tight.

There was an unexpected advantage in losing a child, Jess mused, horrified at the appalling truth. She would never voice such a sentiment aloud, but now that Tyler was gone and the house was quiet of an evening, she and Steve had finally been able to catch up on all the TV shows people always talked about, which they'd never had time to watch.

Jess was an awful person, she knew that, but at least now she'd binged every season of *The White Lotus* and *Better Call Saul*. She was in love with Cillian Murphy. She knew that *Fleabag* and *The Crown* were not for her. *Westworld* went whooshing right over her head. Steve's favourite turned out to be *Bojack Horseman*. Jess assumed it was because he identified with the pathetic, alcoholic equine protagonist.

That was where Steve would be at that moment. Day-drunk in front of the plasma with Baz Luhrmann snoring next to him.

Later, Jess would carry him to bed and try not to feel pity for the man. She wondered how many other partners had done the same; how many had quietly quit their jobs and lost themselves in booze, or drugs, how many had taken their own lives?

Voices were raised at the back of the library, settling down as abruptly as they'd come. A group of intellectually disabled teenagers were watching a video in the company of their carer. Jess browsed the flyers promoting library events. Baby Rhyme Time. Free Food Fridays. Yoga and Mindfulness. The Rubik's Cube Club. An author Zoom interview. No mention of anything O9 related. *So much for being a community hub*, Jess thought. It was as if the event had never happened. As if it wasn't still happening.

'Excuse me, your computer is ready,' a librarian called. 'Number three, please.'

'I notice you're not running any support groups for Orpheans,' Jess said.

The librarian's cheeks flushed. She raised a hand halfway to her mouth then caught herself.

'No,' she said, slowly and carefully. 'We asked but were told mental health services are beyond our remit.'

'Who told you that?' Jess asked, annoyed not so much by the lack of services as by the manner in which the librarian regarded her, as if she was some kind of plague carrier. Orpheans were sometimes treated the same as those who had dared to cough in public during Covid. Everyone backed away slowly, staring at them as if they should be isolated from the general populace.

'A representative from the shire,' the librarian said. 'If it were up to us we'd of course try to help, but it's a point of contention at council. If you're keen to advocate for a support group, maybe attend one of the public meetings and raise the issue.'

Jess held up her hands to show she wasn't trying to start a beef.

'Maybe I'll try the Rubik's Cube Club instead,' she said.

'Yes!' the librarian said, clearly relieved. 'They have an expert who solves them in thirty seconds.'

'Must be short meetings,' Jess muttered. 'Computer three, you say?'

'Yes,' the librarian said. 'Obviously there are restrictions on viewing certain sites, just FYI.'

'I'm not here to watch porn,' Jess told her.

'No, but I've heard the government are cracking down on some forums,' the librarian said, smiling apologetically.

'God forbid citizens might harbour thoughts of insurrection,' Jess said. 'Thanks, I'll be careful.'

Jess sat at the computer and logged in using her library account. *They can track me*, she thought.

After browsing mindlessly for a while, she typed in the web address Georgia Slater had sent her. The unrestricted page opened on a subreddit account called OrpheanMoms. As Jess filtered through the discussions and comments, a smile slowly crossed her face. These were her people. Honest. Forthcoming. Strident. Disgruntled.

Jess settled on a conversation between three American users and read back through the thread.

Kandi77: Bad news, I'm afraid. Remember my friend Tamara? She used to post here as wyldwood. She's gone. Not dead, at least not as far as I know, but they took her. She wasn't answering her phone and I got worried, so I drove three hundred miles to check on her. The apartment was empty, like she'd moved out, but when I spoke to one of the neighbours, they told me a white van turned up one morning and they bundled her into the back. Someone came a few days later and cleaned the place out. Took me a while to find her. She's in an Orpheanage upstate, an old asylum the state has repurposed to house O9 trauma victims deemed to be a menace to society. What a joke. We're back to the days of branding women as hysterical and pumping them full of drugs. I want to visit and see if she's ok but I'm worried that if I apply for a permit, their attention might fall upon me. I'm probably not as far gone as Tammy was. She was really struggling to cope and there was that incident at CVS where she got tased after handing out flyers. Any ideas about how we can find out what's happening in the Orpheanages? Back doors into their systems? There must be a way we can access their records. We don't even know how many women they've detained. It's got to be illegal, right?

Ghostrabbit: Actually, it's not. Most states have passed legislation granting the Department of Health extraordinary powers to intervene and apprehend women they view as presenting a threat to the hegemony. I'm sorry to hear about your friend, Kandi77, but it doesn't surprise me. This sort of thing is happening with alarming frequency, and not just in the US. If only we lived in Sweden, where at least they're allocating an equal number of resources to caring for Orpheans as they are to trying to prevent more waves.

Surgeongeneral: Not that it will make any difference, Ghostrabbit. Authorities everywhere are so far behind the eight ball on this one. They're scrabbling for solutions, and in the meantime more kids are dying. You heard the latest crap about vaccines coming out of Canada?

Kandi77: Vaccines aren't feasible. O9 isn't a virus. It's more like a supernatural event.

Surgeongeneral: You may be right, but that's not stopping them from pumping trillions of dollars into Big Pharma so they can develop a jab that will achieve sweet fuck-all.

Ghostrabbit: What are they claiming this vaccine will do?

Surgeongeneral: It's supposed to block the recombinant DNA matrix, fooling the disease into thinking kids are older.

Ghostrabbit: That sounds like BS. And it's not a disease. This won't work.

Surgeongeneral: Right? But they're going ahead with it anyway. Get ready for an even greater polarisation of society when they offer a rushed, untested solution to the parents of every eight-year-old, who'll be so desperate to try it they'll gloss over the potential long-term effects.

Kandi77: Back to Orpheanages. Any advice?

Surgeongeneral: I'd be careful talking about that subject openly on these forums, Kandi77. They know who all the Orpheans are. They keep a register. There's too many of us for them to round up, but they'll have red flag keyword searches and if your name pings too many times . . . let's just say if a white van pulls up outside, go out the back way and start running. Hit me on the private WhatsApp group and I'll see if I can hook you up with someone who knows a back door into their system.

Those places were set up in a hurry, so their servers aren't locked down as tightly as they should be.

Kandi77: Thanks, SG. I'll light a candle for Lauren. And one for Malik too, Ghostrabbit.

Surgeongeneral: . . . I miss her so much. Love you both.

Ghostrabbit: You're in our prayers, Kandi. Your Elijah is with them in heaven. Stay strong.

After reading just that one short thread, Jess felt better informed and more connected than she had since Tyler's death. The real world was slow and listless and judgemental, and mean. Online, women like her were engaged in frank discussions about the challenges facing people *just like them*. Jess felt buoyed with a sense of hope and potential she hadn't experienced for years. As an Orphean she was part of something, part of a movement.

Of course, the government didn't want Orpheans congregating. If they did, *those women* would find a way to channel their fury, to demand action. To ask for recompense, for justice. Anger bubbled within, clawing its way up Jess's spine. Tyler, her son, whom she loved more than anything in the whole cruel world, was dead. And someone was responsible. O9 didn't just appear out of thin air. The event was calculated. It had to be. The kids sang the Latin translation of a quote from *King Lear*, for fuck's sake. Someone was behind it – a person, or group of people. And they had to be held to account. They had to pay for what they did, what they were still doing, inflicting this tsunami of torture.

Jess typed Australia into the search bar on the subreddit and was rewarded with several pages of conversation between Orpheans in her part of the world. The only way for her to make an impact was by keeping it local. News of riots and massacres and extreme government measures elsewhere in the world were omnipresent in news media, but there was no room for that in Jess's head. She lived in Gattan, a backwater town at the arse end of the world that no one cared about. But she was there, and there were others just like her. She'd often see them, wandering the streets like spectres caught between this world and the next.

Jess, grief-stricken and incensed, scanned the Australian threads until something caught her eye. Reclaim your Kingdom. A link for those who wanted to act in Gattan, for those who were ready to fight back.

Jess Ward clicked on the link and a new window opened. There was no text, just a black background and a pulsing red trident.

PART TWO

THE SALTLESS

HAYLEY CARLISLE KNEW HER DAUGHTER WAS RUNNING OUT OF time. Ebony Carlisle-Tan was eight years old. Hayley could practically hear the seconds passing. *Tick. Tick. Tick.* But Hayley knew if she dwelled on the force drawing Ebony inexorably towards her ninth birthday, neither of them would be able to function. They had to continue with daily life as if nothing was going to happen. Ignore the fact that one day, many months down the track, Ebony would come shuddering to a halt and burst into song, moments before her body swelled with sodium chloride, turning her into a balloon animal who would die within minutes.

Maintaining order was important. Hayley firmly believed that scientists, doctors and governments would find a solution long before the hands of the clock swept towards 11 am on Ebony's birthday. But, in the meantime, she would do whatever was necessary to preserve some semblance of normalcy in her child's life. She would also do everything in her power to exempt her daughter from the mysterious cull, just in case.

Hayley parked her RAV4 hybrid in one of the two-hour spots behind Tyrepower on Watt Street and walked to Dropzone, toting a box of thirty-six seed and nut bars. Hayley was extremely proud of her contribution to fighting the O9 scourge. Her home-baked Freelance bars contained no salt, hence the name, which she thought was very smart. It was an anagram of NaCl Free, with an added 'e'. Her customers merely nodded politely when she explained its meaning, not half as impressed by Hayley's cleverness as she was. Having to explain that NaCl was the chemical annotation for sodium chloride really dulled the impact.

She ordered an oat chai latte and waited for the manager, Robbie, to emerge. When he did, he had a tea towel draped over one shoulder. Hayley found this unhygienic but shook his hand anyway.

'Resupply?' Robbie said.

'Yes. These ones have acai berries.'

Robbie nodded. The café was busy. He glanced at the harried barista, wreathed in a cloud of steam.

'Yeah, good,' Robbie said. 'They're going quite well. How's Ebony?'

He regretted the question the second it escaped his lips. Hayley was one of the Saltless. They were considered cult adjacent, well on the path to becoming a fully fledged religion.

'I found an empty bag of Twisties in her coat pocket last week,' Hayley said. 'She won't listen. The salt content in those is off the charts. Did you know the average person consumes three and a half thousand milligrams of sodium each day? That's three times the recommended amount. Seventy per cent of that comes from pre-packaged foods. If we cut those out and concentrate on an organic, natural diet, we're already dramatically improving the odds of survival.' Her voice grew louder. 'It's irresponsible of Woolworths to even sell such garbage. Chips and all other pre-packaged foods with high sodium content should be banned. What's wrong with people? This is such an obvious contributing cause to the crisis.'

Robbie glanced at his other customers, several of whom were looking askance at Hayley.

'We try to avoid salt wherever possible here,' he said, eager to wind up the conversation. 'Clogs the arteries, my mum always said,' he added, trying to be light-hearted.

'Exactly!' Hayley was on a roll. 'And yet you hear people saying that we're denying our children an essential ingredient for their development. They're in the pockets of Big Salt! That's a powerful lobby group. The fact is, humans barely need salt at all. The body requires less than five hundred milligrams a day to function properly. That's not even a quarter of a teaspoon. No wonder kids are dying from kidney failure. Their little systems are full of this toxic substance.'

'Yeah, like I said, we don't even have it on the tables,' Robbie tried to interject.

'We may not understand much about O9, but surely it makes practical sense to mitigate excess sodium. I've seen reports of mums who've saved their children by successfully eliminating salt from their diet. You can't tell me it's not worth trying to give my daughter a fighting chance.'

'Well, hey, look, Hayley, I've got to get back to it but thanks for coming in,' Robbie said, clutching the box of Freelance bars to his chest. 'Send me an invoice and we'll work out what I owe you.'

'Thanks, Robbie,' she said, a hot flush spreading across her chest as she realised several of the older patrons in the café were staring at her like she was insane.

'Oat chai for Hayley,' the barista said, placing her takeaway on the counter. She sipped it as she walked back to the car. Hayley was accustomed to pointed stares of disapproval. They didn't bother her. She knew the Saltless moniker was intended as a pejorative, a slightly disdainful label used in small, conservative regional towns – usually delivered with the same eye roll that accompanied descriptors like coeliac, vegan or Greens voter. Hayley didn't give a fig. Being salt free made sense, from a biologically holistic point of view. She didn't invent the statistics she had quoted to Robbie. That was hard science.

Hayley's next port of call was the health food shop on Reed Street. At least there, she would be guaranteed a sympathetic ear.

The window of Gattan Health Foods was adorned with an array of stickers and flyers blu-tacked to the glass: Save Boyd Creek. Stop Sand Mining. Save Coronet State Forest. Squeeze your own olive oil. Save the Powerful Owl. Ayurvedic Yoga Retreat. Protect the Grassland Earless Dragon. And there, amongst the worthy causes, a homemade sign that read: Saltless Friendly. Hayley slid open the door and entered the tiny shop.

Hayley breathed deeply upon entering the health food store. The decision to live a salt-free lifestyle had rendered grocery shopping difficult. Here was a place where dietary requirements were understood and, more than that, respected. The owner, Deb Tonkin, stood behind the counter, scratching her head as she pored over invoices. She glanced up at Hayley and gave her a welcoming smile.

'If it isn't our famous local Saltfluencer,' Deb said. 'How are you, mate?'

'Pretty good,' Hayley said, handing over the box. 'I brought you some more Freelance bars.'

'Great, we're almost out,' Deb said. 'Might have to increase my order.'

While this was a thrill for Hayley to hear, it also filled her with trepidation. More orders was a stark reminder that she wasn't the only parent desperately trying to save their child. There were millions just like her, and hundreds in Gattan. It also meant more late nights in the kitchen. She was a one-woman operation. As the primary earner in the family, Jude had zero interest in doing anything of an evening other than crashing on the couch and rewatching old episodes of *It's Always Sunny in Philadelphia*. Ebony gave her a hand sometimes, but she could be more of a liability than a help.

'I might pick up a few things while I'm here,' Hayley said, eyeing off the scoop bins of gluten-free pasta and wholemeal rice.

Hayley had removed all pre-packaged and high salt content foods from her pantry. They no longer had condiments. No soy sauce, no dips, no mustard, no olives in jars, no peanut butter, no jam, no Nutella, no ketchup, no salad dressing and no mayonnaise. And she didn't trust labelling that claimed a product was low in salt. They had no canned soups, vegetables or fruits. Absolutely no junk food. Lollies, chocolate, biscuits, cookies and chips – especially chips – were banned.

She scooped a kilogram of dried chickpeas into a paper bag.

'Did you know canned chickpeas contain forty per cent more sodium than freshly picked?' Deb asked.

'Unbelievable.' Hayley sighed. 'We mostly eat grilled or roasted veggies now. A lot of eggs.'

'Basically paleo,' Deb said.

Hayley shook her head. 'No meat. We respect the sentience of animals in our house. The biggest problem is breakfast. I've tried weaning Ebony onto a savoury breakfast, but she hates it. She wants cereal and yoghurt. Those are no-go areas. Hidden salt content. I make my own granola, but she only eats a few mouthfuls. My worry is that she's exposed to salted foods at school.'

'You seen that new Saltless aisle in Coles?' Deb asked. 'They're acting like they're sensitive to their customers' needs, but they're just cashing in.'

'I wouldn't trust those products anyway,' Hayley said. 'At least we live in the country and have access to fresh food. Up in the city, it's a different story. The supermarkets have some things but not others. Every time Jude has to work in the office, she says it's impossible to eat healthy.'

'Tell me about it,' Deb said. 'I have a list the length of your arm of items I just can't get anymore due to supply chain issues. Is Jude back in there full time?'

Hayley shook her head. 'It varies, but she usually works from home a couple of days a week. It's such a long commute.'

'Yeah, I never go to the city anymore,' Deb said. 'Especially now. Apparently, you can't get an ambulance because they're always attending to . . . shit, sorry, Hayley, I wasn't thinking.'

'That's okay,' Hayley said. 'There's still plenty of time for us. I'm confident a solution will be found before it's too late. I have to be, you know?'

'Sure,' Deb said. 'I'm not convinced it has a one hundred per cent mortality rate anyway. I've heard whispers of parents saving their kids.'

'Yes!' Hayley said. 'I heard that too. If you go hardcore saltless, or isolate the child completely, that can work.'

It was only an hour until school pick-up time so rather than go home, Hayley decided to hang around town. There wasn't much to see in Gattan. The town was a three-hour drive from the city and had no train line. If it weren't for the big box stores, no one would ever go there. Jude's city friends often confessed they had no idea where it was, and some hadn't even heard of the place. Hayley would joke that Gattan enjoyed a rich cultural life because they had a McDonald's and a KFC. McDonald's grand gesture towards corporate responsibility was their Salt-Free burger. Hayley tried one when they were first released. It wasn't great, and the taste made her suspect that it wasn't salt-free either.

Gattan was on the way to somewhere else. Visitors stopped for fuel and coffee and to use the public toilets before heading to one of the shiny villages on the coast, where seagulls would swoop in and steal their hot chips, assuming they could find a place that still served them. On the rare occasion someone from the city expressed an interest in making a sea change,

Hayley would dissuade them by proudly claiming Gattan had the finest crystal methamphetamine in the state, primo product that would knock the teeth right out of your mouth. Ironically, it was true.

After browsing the musty second-hand bookstore for a while, Hayley found herself back in the car and parked outside the school. She was early but that was on purpose in case Ebony's class was given an early mark. With each passing day, Hayley's saltless resolve hardened in line with the unthinkable, paralysing fear that nothing would change, that wave after wave of Orpheus Nine would claim its innocent victims, that every child under nine was doomed, that *her* child was doomed, that it would never end. Hayley's inner turmoil was real, focused and ever-present and she needed to cling on to every moment she could get with her daughter. She sat in silence, gripping the steering wheel; she was holding it together the only way she knew how – by believing she could make a difference. That she could change the story.

After the bell, Ebony came running out alongside her friends, laughing and chatting merrily, as if they weren't all fated to die over the coming months. Hayley switched on the ignition, lowered the window and waved to her daughter.

Ebony hugged her friends and told them she'd see them tomorrow. A chill traversed Hayley's spine as she realised there would be times when that would not be true. There had been two deaths already in Ebony's class. There would be more.

Ebony opened the door and jumped in the back seat of the Toyota.

'Have a nice day at school?' Hayley asked, peering at her daughter in the rear-view.

'Uh-huh,' Ebony said, looking guilty. She was terrible at concealing her emotions. Hayley could practically read her daughter's thoughts.

Hayley unclipped her seatbelt, got out of the car and slid into the back seat beside her daughter. Ebony was alarmed, but she knew what was coming. Hayley frisked her thoroughly, patting her daughter down. She made her turn out her pockets, take off her shoes, lift her jumper and skirt. Hayley opened her schoolbag and searched it, emptying books, pencil case and lunch box onto the leather seat.

'Where is it?' Hayley demanded.

Ebony shrugged as if she had no idea what her mother was talking about. She squirmed on the seat uncomfortably, and Hayley heard a crinkling sound.

'Take it out, or I'll make you pull your undies down right here in the school car park,' Hayley said.

Ebony puffed out her cheeks and reached up under her dress to pull a crumpled bag of Cheezels out of her underwear. Hayley snatched it from her. Most of the chips had been eaten. Those that remained had largely been crushed into yellow dust.

'I was saving them for later,' Ebony protested.

'Who gave these to you?' Hayley asked.

Ebony shook her head, her lips firmly pressed together. She was no snitch.

The eight-year-old flinched when her mother raised an open hand to slap her across the face. But Hayley held back, grinding her teeth and slowly clenching her fingers into a fist that she carefully lowered. She wasn't there yet, but she knew the precipice was fast approaching.

* * *

Hey, what's up everybody? I'm Hayley and welcome to the latest reel of Saltless4Lyf. Thank you all so much for watching and remember, if you like what you see today, hit the heart icon or leave a comment. I'd love to hear what you think, except, you know, please be respectful.

I was thinking about family Christmases and how this year that joyous day of coming together in celebration will have a dark cloud hanging over it – unless O9 is gone before then, and fingers crossed that'll be the case! Even so, lots of you out there will have experienced heartbreaking loss or be close to someone who has, and so today I decided to make a sweet saltless treat that is not only reminiscent of Christmas but that is also guaranteed to raise the spirits. I'll be showing you how to make your very own Saltless Ferrero Rocher powerballs.

These treats are also free of refined sugars, gluten and oil and they're vegan, so ideal for virtually every dietary requirement. The only equipment you'll need is a food processor, but a blender will work too, if you don't mind a little elbow grease. Best of all, these sweet beauties only take five minutes to make, and can be kept in the fridge for days, although be warned: they won't last that long!

All right, so let's talk ingredients. You'll need roughly half a cup of roasted hazelnuts and a few more set aside for the centres. Pulse the hazelnuts and add a quarter cup of gluten-free rolled oats or oatmeal flour until you get this grainy texture. You see that? Don't overwork them. Next, you add eight Medjool dates. Make sure you pit these first, and if you want to speed up the process, slice the dates into pieces. Just scoop them in there like that, there you go. Now, you also want to add a quarter cup of almonds here – again, you can chop them up first to make it easy. Add three teaspoons of cacao powder. Please make sure this has zero salt. Some brands will try to fool you, so it pays to read the label. Scrape half a vanilla pod into the mix, rather than using vanilla essence, which again, isn't always trustworthy. Finally, to hold the mixture together we need two tablespoons of almond butter. This is where it's easy to come unstuck. A lot of almond butter contains traces of salt, so shop around and check with your local independent health food retailer.

If you're struggling to source saltless butters and spreads, I'm including a link below to Dove Grinders Sodium Free range. Their products are gorgeous and it's a small company run by a Saltless couple, so I highly recommend you check them out.

As you can see, we now have our dough. All you have to do is scoop it out – and you can use your hands here, as long as they're clean – press one of the whole hazelnuts you set aside into the mixture, then roll it into a ball like so. And there you have it! One saltless knock-off Ferrero Rocher. Yum! Wrap them in foil and serve them on a silver platter like you're visiting the Italian Embassy, or I recommend piling them on a plate in the refrigerator and watching as they disappear! The perfect healthy treat to pack in your little one's lunch box.

Thanks for watching and don't forget to like and comment below. I'm Hayley, and this is Saltless4Lyf!

* * *

HAYLEY TURNED TO HER PARTNER WHEN THE VIDEO ENDED.

'Too much at the end?' she asked.

'Nah, it's good,' Jude said. 'How many takes until you got it right?'

'Only three this time,' Hayley said. 'I stuffed up Dove Grinders the first time, then almost choked on an almond on the second take. I'm getting better, though.'

'Make sure you include all the hashtags,' Jude suggested, scrolling through Hayley's previous posts on her own phone. 'You're up to twenty-six thousand followers now, eh?'

'More all the time,' Hayley said. 'It's a real community.'

Jude stretched, yawned and put her feet up on the pouf. She reached for the remote control.

'You going to stay here and watch something with me?' Jude asked. 'Last night's episode of *Have You Been Paying Attention?* is on 10Play.'

'I'd love to, I could do with a laugh,' Hayley said. 'But I should probably bake. I've had a few extra orders this week.'

'I'd offer to help but, you know, I don't want to,' Jude said.

'Really? I hadn't noticed your antipathy.'

'Ask Eb,' Jude said.

Hayley shook her head. 'She's on lockdown,' she said.

'Because of the Cheezels?' Jude raised an eyebrow. 'You need to go easy on her, babe. She's only a kid.'

'You know why I'm hard on her,' Hayley said, struggling to find the right words. She didn't want to sound cold-hearted. 'Her time may be limited.'

Jude winced.

'You think I don't know that? It has me up nights, pacing the house, wondering if we should retreat to the Kerguelen Islands, where the fucking thing can't reach her.'

'The Kerguelen Islands?' Hayley asked.

'Sub-Antarctic,' Jude explained. 'Also known as the Desolation Islands. About as far away from civilisation as it's possible to get.'

Hayley nodded, trying to imagine herself decamping to a tiny windswept island at the bottom of the world. As if Gattan wasn't isolated enough. Jude placed a hand on her thigh.

'Listen, in the event of the worst-case scenario approaching, we'll do something,' she said. 'We'll run, rent a boat, take to the open ocean. Hijack a fucking rocket and head for Mars if we have to. But in the meantime, you've got to let her live a little.'

'What if letting her live condemns her to death?' Hayley said.

Jude buried her face in her hands. 'I don't know,' she said. 'I don't have the answers. No one does.'

'I'll think about it,' Hayley said. She rubbed Jude's arm. 'I need to bake. Try not to fall asleep out here.'

Hayley popped her head around the door of her daughter's room before heading into the kitchen. Ebony was lying face down across the bed, propped up on her elbows. Her features were illuminated by the screen of her iPad. Hayley had resisted the device as long as she could, but Ebony and Jude wore her down. It was tough limiting screen time when your daughter was a prisoner in her own room.

'I'm baking some Freelance bars,' Hayley said. 'You want to come out and help?'

Ebony's side-eye had recently ascended to Olympic level.

'I'm watching *One Piece*,' she said. Hayley frowned. 'It's a fantasy show based on a comic,' Ebony elaborated. 'It's fine, don't worry.'

'You were typing when I came in,' Hayley said.

'My friends and I talk about the show while we're watching it,' she said. 'Since you won't let me go to anyone's house.'

'I guess that's a no to baking, then,' Hayley said.

Ebony ignored her mother, who retreated and shut the door behind her. She clattered around in the kitchen for a while, prepping ingredients, then realised she didn't have enough Tupperware to store the bars. She checked the time on her phone and grabbed her car keys.

'You going out?' Jude called.

'Kmart's still open,' Hayley said. 'I need more containers. Won't be long.'

Jude waved a hand in farewell.

Hayley avoided the shopping plaza as much as possible, but if she had to go, late evening was the optimum time. The cafés and cheap discount stores were shuttered. Bakers Delight was closed. Hayley's gaze fell on the poster pinned to the wall beside the bakery. A memorial photograph of Melanie Whalen, their employee, who had committed suicide after the loss of her daughter. Hayley hurried past.

Kmart beckoned at the end of the plaza. She nodded to the teenager working on the front entrance and made her way to the homewares section, which was surprisingly decent. Hayley was browsing for environmentally friendly storage solutions when she practically stumbled into Jessica Ward. They stared at each other for a few seconds, trapped in an interminably awkward silence that Hayley could not bear. She folded and took the high road.

'Hey, Jess,' she said. 'Haven't seen you around much lately.' Hayley immediately regretted her clumsiness. 'Sorry.'

Jess looked Hayley up and down with detached curiosity.

'All good,' she said. 'Didn't expect to see you in here. Bit beneath you, I'd have thought.'

'No way,' Hayley said. 'They've got some great stuff, although some of these shelves are decimated. People are prepping like it's the apocalypse.'

'How's Ebony?' Jess asked, tapping her wrist even though she wasn't wearing a watch. 'You get her one of those freshwater mermaid dolls yet? I hear they're all the rage with your lot.'

Hayley gritted her teeth and refused to take the bait. 'I'm struggling to get through to her, to be honest,' she said. 'I don't think she truly grasps what's happening.'

'Still got a while, though, right?' Jess said.

Hayley nodded.

'That's rough,' Jess said. 'The waiting. I wouldn't have been able to stand it. Maybe the first wavers lucked out.'

Hayley was shocked by Jess's candour. It terrified her, imagining that the dishevelled woman standing before her might be a vision of her own future.

'How's Steve?' Hayley asked.

'Oh, you know him,' Jess said, waving a hand dismissively.

'Never needed much excuse to dive into a bottle,' Hayley said, immediately regretting the comment, thinking that was it, she'd gone too far. Jess raised an eyebrow.

'Bloody oath,' she said. 'Useless prick.'

It had always puzzled Hayley that Jess married Steve Ward. She hadn't paid him the slightest bit of attention in high school, which was easy because he was so unremarkable. A decent footy player, sure, but hardly the star prop forward. Zero personality. Obsessed with two-stroke engines, to the exclusion of all else. A blink-and-you'd-miss-him country boy.

Jess looked around to check that the coast was clear before leaning in, so close Hayley could smell her deodorant. Rexona. Hayley experienced a moment of fear. Jess was unpredictable.

'Remember when we used to steal fluoro highlighters from here?' Jess said. 'You'd sell them to the farm kids at school.'

'I remember you flashing your undies at the security guard to distract him,' Hayley said.

Jess doubled over, cackling. The sound of her distinctive laugh transported Hayley back to their days of misspent youth, malingering on a wooden bench by the bus stop.

'I miss you, mate,' Hayley said impulsively, which she knew was crossing an unspoken line. Jess stopped laughing and stepped back, blinking, seeming embarrassed that she had moved so close to her former friend.

'Yeah, right,' Jess said. 'I don't think about you at all.'

Hayley stiffened. This was how it went between them. Scathing belittlement, with an undertone of misplaced resentment.

'If you ever need to talk to someone,' Hayley said, 'I can recommend a therapist, or a yoga teacher. Might do you good.'

Jess was formulating a reply when Hayley abruptly accosted the staff member who'd been eyeing them warily from behind the waffle-maker display.

'Excuse me,' Hayley said. 'Can you tell me where the highlighters are?'

Jess glanced sideways at the sixteen-year-old boy.

'Stationery section,' he said. 'Near the kids' stuff.'

'Ah yes,' Hayley said. 'I remember.'

Hayley walked briskly away with a basket full of Tupperware, leaving Jess twitching in the homewares section. The fluorescent highlighters cost nine dollars for a pack of twenty. She added them to her basket. Jess muttered to herself for a moment before stalking out of the store, leaving a basket of goods behind. Hayley took a breath. There was such anger in her old school pal, such nihilism. Hayley knew she should show the Orpheans more empathy, but they made it so difficult, and besides, her hands were full trying not to join their bitter ranks.

* * *

IN THE ABSENCE OF WEEKDAY COMMUTER TRAFFIC, THE HIGHWAY into the city was quiet. Neither Jude nor Ebony was thrilled at being rousted from their respective beds at five-thirty on a cold Saturday morning, but Hayley wanted to arrive early for the protest march. Having already spent two days in the city that week for work, Jude remained sullen for most of the three-hour trip, curled up in the passenger seat of the RAV4, heated seat turned up to max. Ebony dozed in the back, a banner draped across her legs: NA NA NA NA NA SALTMAN! BAN SODIUM CHLORIDE. Hayley would have preferred something more serious but was obliged to resort to comedy to persuade Ebony to come along. Not that she would have left her in the house alone. That presented its own risks. Besides, Hayley thought it best to parade her daughter in public, to show any media in attendance exactly what they were at risk of losing. She knew that many of the other Saltless protesters would also bring their children. The more eight-year-olds on display, the better. They were like Javan rhinos or Amur leopards, fragile species on the verge of extinction.

Jude sat up when they came off the freeway at the riverside exit. She glanced at the GPS.

'Why are we heading for my work?' she asked.

'Free parking,' Hayley said.

'I don't know if that's a good idea,' Jude said. 'We prefer to keep car spaces free for paying patrons on weekends.'

Jude was a curator at one of the museums in the city.

'Don't worry, it's early,' Hayley said. 'We'll be out of there by eleven.'

Hayley knew the real reason for Jude's reluctance was more complex. Her wife was a state government employee and had been told in no uncertain terms that politics and social activism were not appropriate in the workplace. Even Jude's socials were muted. She didn't repost Hayley's articles or photos on the salt crisis, for fear of reprimand.

'I should have worn a mask in case they pick up my face on CCTV,' she said.

'There's a box of them in the glove compartment,' Hayley told her.

'No, like a Halloween mask,' Jude said.

'You want me to let you out on the corner before we park?' Hayley said. 'God forbid you be seen in public giving a shit about your daughter's future.'

'You know I'll stand with you and Ebony,' Jude said. 'I just don't see the point in protesting.'

'There'll be media present. We're forcing these issues onto the public and political agenda,' Hayley said.

'Are we, though?' Jude said. 'It's not like there's anyone who doesn't already know about O9. And forgive me, but I don't think the mayor's going to look out her window at a group of angry protesters and suddenly reassess her entire set of values.'

'And I thought I was cynical,' Hayley said. 'Positive, real-world action is important, Jude.'

'Important for whom?'

'For Ebony, and kids like her.'

'I think you protest because it makes you feel better about yourself,' Jude said. 'You march alongside thousands of people who share the same views, patting each other on the back for being upstanding citizens while berating anyone who doesn't agree with you. It's a form of moral bullying, and it changes nothing.'

'Why do you come, then, if you despise it so much?'

Jude indicated the sleeping kid in the back seat with her thumb.

'For her,' she said. 'I'm so desperate, I'll try anything.'

'We're not so different, after all,' Hayley said.

Jude leant towards her. 'We may not agree on everything, but that's what keeps the fire burning, right, babe?' She kissed Hayley on the cheek. Hayley brushed her off and gripped the steering wheel, but she enjoyed the sensation of Jude's warm lips against her skin.

'I still love you, even though you're a misanthrope,' she told Jude.

'Of course you do,' Jude said.

'You know, there'll be a Saltless Taco truck,' Hayley said.

'Are you serious?' Jude said, sitting bolt upright and whacking the dashboard with her palm. 'You should have led with that. I would've been dragging you out of bed.'

Jude squirmed down in the seat while Hayley found a park in the subterranean garage below the museum, using Jude's swipe card to enter. Ebony yawned and blinked as her mothers extricated her from the vehicle. The girl donned her backpack. Jude and Hayley carried the banner between them.

'If we exit on Johnston, we can walk straight down to the meeting point by the station,' Jude said. 'Plus, the camera at that barrier is on the fritz.'

It was a brisk morning in the city, one of those bright yet cold winter days that fooled you into believing you didn't need a coat, when in fact it took several layers to ward off the chill. The Carlisle-Tan family walked into the heart of the city. Other than a few trucks making early morning deliveries, all was quiet. Most of the shops were yet to open. The family soon noticed others like themselves, wrapped up warm and clutching placards. Mothers, fathers, sons and daughters, gripped by the same debilitating fear of tomorrow.

The protesters congregated in parkland opposite Central Station. The atmosphere soon became animated as attendees conversed and fired each other up. A vibrant surge of energy filtered through the crowd, a mixture of enthusiasm, gratitude and a sense of belonging. Everyone was excited to be there, to be stating their case so boldly and publicly. Complete strangers chatted to Jude and Hayley, expressing anger and sympathy. Ebony writhed in discomfort, unhappy with her involuntary role as an ambassador for the Saltless movement.

'There must be twenty, twenty-five thousand people here,' Jude said, awed by the level of support.

'They can't ignore us,' Hayley said.

The Carlisle-Tans stayed at the rear of the protest as they waited for the organisers to assemble and begin the march over the bridge. Their intention was to block the main junction next to Central Station for at least an hour, to press home their point.

'Cops are here,' Jude said, pointing to a phalanx of uniformed officers on horseback trotting along the boulevard. They were followed by a hundred more on motorcycles. Black militaristic vehicles pulled up by the edge of the park, disgorging hundreds of police in riot gear. Their appearance elicited jeering and boos from the crowd.

'Overkill much?' Jude said. 'Fuckers.'

'Mummy, I'm scared,' Ebony said, slipping her hand into Hayley's.

'It's all right, don't worry,' she told her daughter. 'Stick close to Mummy and me. They're only trying to intimidate us.'

It was working, too. Hayley's stomach was performing a gymnastics floor routine worthy of a podium finish.

'Look at them in their bulletproof vests and wraparound sunnies,' Jude said, pulling her shoulders back like she was spoiling for a fight.

'Jude, dial it down,' Hayley growled, nodding towards their daughter, who was cowering behind her mother's legs.

'Yeah, yeah,' Jude said. 'Just pisses me off, that's all. You'd see less police at a fucking Nazi Party convention.'

'Babe,' Hayley warned her.

'Sorry, sorry,' she said, crouching to fix Ebony's hair. 'It's okay, kiddo. We won't let anything bad happen to you. Mummy's got muscles, remember?'

Jude flexed her arm, which drew a smile from their little girl. She felt Jude's bicep and giggled.

'Hey, you want some churros?' Jude asked her, and glanced up at Hayley.

Ebony's eyes widened.

'Can I?' she asked.

'Let's go take a look,' Hayley said, welcoming the distraction. There was already a short queue at the churros truck, which was plastered with text proclaiming their products as one hundred per cent salt free. It had been several hours since breakfast. Hayley had packed half-a-dozen Freelance bars, but reconsidered at the prospect of a hot, sweet treat instead.

As they ate, the crowd milled towards the main road. Placards and banners were raised. Once they had licked the sugar from their sticky fingers, Hayley and Jude hoisted their own banner aloft. It drew a few confused stares but also a lot of satisfied nods. Ebony held Hayley's hand as they fell into step with the other protesters, marching solemnly out of the park towards the train station under the watchful eye of a police force who had clearly come expecting trouble and who would be disappointed if they went home without encountering any.

The march halted at the junction. Police held back long queues of vehicles, the drivers honking their horns and hurling abuse at the protesters. Members of the public congregated outside Hungry Jack's on the corner opposite the station. The protesters spent ten minutes chanting and swaying, led by a man with a megaphone who called for immediate action, and an investigation into salt levels in commercial products. Hayley, Jude and Ebony lent their voices to the cause, singing enthusiastically. A sense of relief coursed through Hayley. She felt heard.

A group broke away from the crowd and mounted the steps outside the station. The megaphone was handed to a woman wearing a suit. She fumbled with the controls.

'Who's that?' Hayley asked.

'State member, I think,' Jude said. 'Andrea something? I caught a mention of her online. Her son's eight and eleven months. That's him looking terrified by her side.'

The boy peered out across the undulating crowd, tears streaming down his cheeks. Hayley wanted to scoop him up and hold him close, tell him everything was going to be all right.

'That's a disgrace,' a woman standing nearby said. 'She shouldn't be dragging him into this. Imagine using your kid to score political points.'

'Excuse me?' Hayley said to the woman, who had a perm straight out of the eighties. She placed a protective arm around Ebony's shoulders. 'We're doing this for them. It's not about politics, it's about survival.'

The woman's nostrils flared as she looked askance at Ebony.

'You need to let her go,' she said. 'The designs of the gods should not be questioned.'

Hayley baulked. She had no idea what the woman was talking about.

The stranger unfurled a banner of her own and held it high. Around her, several other women did the same. Each of the banners displayed the same symbol: a red trident.

They began chanting.

'Don't look back, don't look back, don't look back . . .'

Jude moved in front of her wife and daughter, pushing them away from the new cell of protesters. A young man amongst them activated a portable speaker. The music that played was a techno track featuring the voice of an actor delivering the fateful lines from *King Lear*.

As flies to wanton boys are we to the gods; They kill us for their sport.

The beat mounted to a crescendo then a throbbing bassline kicked in. The lyrics 'Don't look back' from an old dance track dropped into the mix, and that was when the shoving started.

Saltless parents shouted and pushed at the new arrivals. Someone clawed at the speaker, trying to smash it. Punches were thrown. Alerted to the disturbance in the crowd, several dozen police officers mobilised, using their riot shields and batons to forge an unruly path through the throng. On the steps of the station, the politician was quickly ushered away. The megaphone was handed back to its owner, who called for calm, but his plea was drowned out by a roar of panic.

The stranger pointed a finger at Ebony.

'Let her go!' she shouted. 'You can't stop it. The gods will have her.'

Ebony squealed in terror.

'Jesus fucking Christ,' Hayley said, pulling Ebony close as they were jostled by the crowd.

The woman continued to harangue them. Jude turned to Hayley and gripped her face.

'One second,' she said. 'Stay here. Don't try to stop me.'

'Where are you going?' Hayley asked, clinging to her daughter's arm with all her strength, even though she knew she was probably hurting the child.

Jude cricked her neck and shoved her way through to the counter-protesters. The stranger looked at her with arch bemusement, which vanished when Jude swung an elbow into the woman's righteous face. She crumpled to the ground and was immediately swallowed by the surging mass of bodies. Jude calmly returned to her wife and daughter, and shepherded them towards the steps of the station. Hayley made no comment. She was not an advocate for physical violence, but on this occasion she felt it was justified. And she was proud of her wife for acting so decisively. If Hayley had got her hands on that horrible woman, she would have throttled her.

Behind them, the riot police were swinging their batons with wild abandon, starting as many scuffles as they were dispersing. Their gleeful expressions spoke to a wider frustration. The old world was collapsing. There would be no recriminations for what happened that day, or any other day.

Hayley ducked as a bottle flew overhead. It struck the shields of the riot police and billowed into flame. Several more petrol bombs followed, exploding on the ground and amongst the crowd. Screams rang out and everyone began to run. Jude, Hayley and Ebony sought refuge under the awning of the station, watching for an opportunity to escape.

Hayley hugged Ebony to her as a woman on fire ran into view on the other side of the road. She turned her daughter's head away as the woman flailed wildly, completely ablaze, before stopping in front of Hungry Jack's, perhaps realising that was it, that these were her last precious seconds of life. She swayed, her entire body licked with flame, and raised her right arm, fist tightly clenched. One final act of defiance. Some carrying trident banners cheered in support, although others wept as the woman's arm lowered and she dropped to her knees. She slumped forward and fell, face down on the pavement, and was still.

PART THREE

THE DECADIAN

DESPITE THE CHILL OF THE AFTERNOON, DIRK VAN DER SAAR drove home from work with the window lowered so he could listen to the exhaust note on his bright yellow 1969 Holden Monaro. He didn't always drive the classic to the store, out of concern for the integrity of its bodywork. The errant youth of Gattan, even if they didn't scratch the panels, would at the very least smear their grubby fingers on the doorframe and bonnet while inspecting the plush interior. Dirk also had a hybrid Lexus SUV parked in the garage at home, which was his normal daily driver.

That morning, Dirk had felt ebullient, filled with the promise of better days to come. Sure, he had sympathy for his fellow citizens who had lost children to the scourge, as the months rolled by and the horror of Orpheus Nine continued taking more unabated. But Dirk was strangely, guiltily buoyed by the knowledge that if no solution was found – and this seemed increasingly likely as the powers-that-be floundered – his son Alex would be part of the final generation. A bitter pill for humanity, perhaps, a devastating conclusion to evolution that could drive the world to the brink of ruination, but the blow would be tempered by the fact that a Van der Saar was amongst the survivors who would, upon reaching adulthood, inherit the earth.

Alex van der Saar had made the cut-off with ten days to spare. That pleased Dirk, but it did not surprise him. His family had always landed on their feet. Triumph was in their genes. The Van der Saars overcame whatever obstacles lay in their path and always achieved their goals. They were winners. Young Alex had suffered a cataclysmic trauma, witnessed the deaths of his classmates and then attended their mass funeral. That was a psychological injury that would take years of therapy to heal. But Dirk was confident his son would eventually get over it. That he'd move on and embrace his role as a leader in the new world to come, whatever form it might take.

Dirk pulled into the driveway and pressed the button on his keychain to open the garage door. Lucy's Tesla was plugged into the charger next to his Lexus. He carefully manoeuvred the Monaro into its spot at the rear of the garage and cut the engine, reminding himself to cover the vehicle once the motor had cooled.

Lucy van der Saar collared her husband the moment he stepped through the door.

'It's happening again,' she said. 'The school sent him home early.'

'Who was it this time?' Dirk asked her.

'He won't say. Claims he's not a dobber.'

Dirk had an inkling the bully might be Jayden McAllister. He was older than Alex, and bigger, and his father Bill nursed an old grudge against Dirk because he had briefly dated Bill's wife Lizzy in high school.

'Where is he now?' Dirk asked.

'In his room,' Lucy said. 'I called his counsellor, but she can't see him until Saturday.'

'Not much use to us, then, is she?' Dirk said. 'I'll have a word with him.'

A suggestion to go easy danced on Lucy's lips but remained unspoken. Dirk threw his keys into the bowl on the sideboard and walked the length of the house to his son's bedroom. He knocked on the door before entering. This was a recently acquired habit, after Lucy had almost walked in on her son while he was exploring his nascent sexuality.

'It's open,' Alex called out.

'Hey, mate,' Dirk said, opening the door a crack. 'All right if I come in for a bit?'

'Sure,' Alex said.

The boy showed no signs of distress. Dirk half expected him to be moping on his bed, face plunged into a tear-soaked pillow, but instead, he was lounging in his gaming chair, immersed in a PlayStation game. Dirk chewed on his lip, resisting the urge to tell his son to turn that fucking thing off. He had learnt that the best method for dealing with Alex's gaming obsession was to feign interest, even participate on occasion. He and Alex had consequently sunk hours together on lazy Sunday afternoons teaming up to kill whoever crossed their path in *Fortnite*. Dirk preferred *Call of Duty: Modern Warfare*. He found *Fortnite* too bubble-gum bright, and the game to be populated by loudmouth dickheads.

Alex was playing *God of War: Ragnarok*. Dirk spent a moment watching him and marvelling at the graphics.

'Looks better than the first one,' he said. 'And that was good.'

Alex nodded and glanced up at his father.

'Just a sec,' he said.

While Dirk waited for his son to finish decimating elves with the axe of Kratos, he looked around the bedroom. It was neat and tidy. He had Alex well drilled in that regard. A schoolbag sat on the chair, unopened. Dirk made a mental note to make sure the kid didn't fall behind on his homework. Bullies or no, he didn't want Alex to miss the golden opportunity that was unfolding before him.

Alex paused the game and slipped off his headset.

'Sorry,' he said. 'Hey, Dad.'

'Heard you were sent home again,' Dirk said, trying to sound nonchalant.

'Yup,' Alex said, fiddling with the controller.

'Jayden McAllister, yeah?'

Alex shrugged.

'Reckon I might drop by the principal's office in the morning and have a word,' Dirk said.

Alex's eyes went wide.

'Don't, Dad,' he said. 'Please.'

'Never beg, Alex,' Dirk said, barely masking his disgust. 'You're a Van der Saar. We built this town.'

'You'll make it worse,' Alex told his father.

'In that case, you need to sort it out,' Dirk said.

'I know.'

'Pick the ringleader,' Dirk told him. 'McAllister himself. Don't be intimidated by his size. Lash out. Laugh when he hits you but don't lie down, keep coming back at him. Make him think you're crazy. None of them will bother you after that.'

'It's not that easy,' Alex said.

'I know, son,' Dirk said, moving to rub his son's shoulders. 'But the only thing boys like that respect is strength, and it doesn't have to be physical. Adults are the same. If they fear you, they'll follow you. If you're not the alpha, then you're someone's bitch.

It's up to you, son, but remember, you were the last one standing on that oval. That means something.'

Alex took a deep breath and nodded. Dirk knew his advice probably stood in stark contrast to what the boy was hearing from his touchy-feely counsellor, but he was his father, and he knew best. He could not countenance the Van der Saar name being dragged through the mud by a bunch of pre-teens who thought they were gangsters because they listened to Post Malone. If need be, Dirk would wait for them to come out of school and sort them out personally. He had no tolerance for bullies.

'You up for a quick run along the nature trail before dinner?' he suggested.

'Definitely,' Alex said, replacing his headset.

'I'll fetch you in thirty,' Dirk said. 'Good talk, bro.'

They fist-bumped and Alex restarted his game.

Dirk practically walked into his daughter in the corridor outside his son's room.

'Eavesdropping again?' he said. 'That's a bad habit, mate.'

'You should hear yourself,' Sky said. 'He's only ten and you're talking to him like he's in prison.'

'School is prison,' Dirk said. 'Was for me, anyway. Don't reckon it's changed much.'

'All that talk about being an alpha is toxic, Dad,' Sky said. 'Alex will turn out to be a woman-hating incel if you keep that up.'

'He's going to be the last of us,' Dirk said. 'Maybe one of the last humans ever born if this crap keeps up. He needs to process that.'

'I can't believe you'd exploit a disaster for your advantage,' Sky said. 'You honestly think millions of kids dying can be turned to your benefit?'

'It's a positive spin.' Dirk laughed.

'It's callous and mercenary,' Sky told him.

'What do you want me to do, Sky? Mope around feeling sorry for all the poor bastards who've lost their kids? I still have mine. We should be grateful. You should be grateful. What I said to Alex counts for you, too. You're the final generation. Don't you get what that means?'

Sky shook her head.

'They'll find a cure or some way to stop it,' she said.

'Don't be so sure,' Dirk said. 'They're none the wiser now, months down the line, than they were when it first happened.'

'A little empathy wouldn't go amiss,' Sky said.

'For whom? The Orpheans? Walking streaks of misery.'

'What about all the eight-year-olds?' Sky said. 'Imagine living that nightmare.'

An image of Ebony as a toddler bouncing on his knee flashed across Dirk's synapses. He couldn't bear to think about anything happening to Hayley and Jude's kid.

'Just because it didn't affect us, we can't pretend like it's not happening,' Sky continued.

'There's a harsh lesson you need to learn, Sky,' Dirk interrupted. 'If you try to carry all the world's problems on your shoulders, pretty soon you'll sink into the mud. Choose your battles, mate. Your grandmother used to have a tea towel that said, "God grant me the serenity to accept the things I cannot change, the courage to change those I can, and the wisdom to know the difference." Wise words.'

'Wow, now you're dispensing tea-towel advice. So you're saying I should just move on?' Sky frowned. 'Ignore the plight of anyone less fortunate than myself? Accept my privilege and not use it to help others?'

'Explain to me how posting to the echo chamber on Instagram helps others,' Dirk said, folding his arms.

'I'm spreading the word,' Sky said.

'No, you're not,' Dirk told her. 'Performative activism changes nothing; it just makes you feel like a better person. You're not actually helping anyone affected by Orpheus Nine.'

Sky considered this for a moment.

'Well, if it's between that and being a self-centred narcissistic sociopath like you, my conscience is clear,' she said.

Dirk couldn't help smirking. He was proud that Sky had turned out so clever and full of opinions, that they could engage in such robust discussions without resorting to rancour.

'We're running along the nature trail in about twenty,' he said.

'I heard,' Sky replied.

'You coming?'

Sky sighed and shrugged.

'I guess so,' she said.

'Still got that competitive streak, eh?' Dirk pretended to punch his daughter on the arm. 'That's my girl.'

Sky batted his fist away. 'Fuck off, you psycho.'

Dirk spent the next ten minutes half listening to his wife recount her day, nodding at the appropriate moments while he played on his phone. He got changed into his running gear then met his progeny on the deck.

The nature trail passed by the rear of their home, stretching three kilometres in each direction. It was rarely frequented. Dirk only ever saw a man who looked like Kevin Rudd walking four identical terriers and the occasional tradie on an e-bike taking a shortcut through to the industrial estate.

The light was already fading when they set off on their run along the dirt trail. They kept up a fast pace. Dirk streaked ahead, although lately Sky had been keeping up. Dirk knew she would soon outpace him, and he was glad for that. He wanted his daughter to be a leader. There was no room for slackers in the Van der Saar clan.

They were halfway along the trail when Dirk spotted a man with a stepladder under his arm emerging from dense bushland ahead.

He was carrying something else in the other hand. The young man panicked when he spotted them approaching, but he had nowhere to go. He stood, immobile, by the side of the trail and waited for the joggers to pass, averting his gaze when they did, so they could not see his face.

When they reached the end of the trail, the trio stopped to rest before the return leg.

'Did you see what that man had under his arm?' Sky asked.

'Looked like a package,' Dirk said, doubled over, catching his breath.

'It was a koala,' Alex said, red-faced.

'Not a real one,' Sky added. 'A fake.'

'What was he doing with it?' Alex asked.

'Drugs,' Sky said.

Dirk shot her a warning glance.

'That's where they keep the meth,' she explained. 'So I heard, anyway.'

Alex was confused. Despite the adult nature of the topic, Dirk felt compelled to explain. He didn't want his son growing up naïve.

'They stuff the koala full of drugs and hide it in the bush,' he said. 'That way if the police raid their property, they won't find anything.'

Alex laughed. 'A drug koala!'

Sky matched her father's exasperated expression.

'This town,' she said. 'Remind me why we live here?'
'We've always lived here,' Dirk said. 'It's our home.'

* * *

VENUS CREEK WAS AN UNHERALDED SINGLE-STREET HAMLET located just off the main highway into Gattan. It was situated along a potholed back road littered with the flattened carcasses of rabbits and the occasional unlucky fox. There were no shops in Venus Creek, only an old butter factory that had closed in the 1940s. An enterprising visitor from the city had bought the building several years prior with the intention of converting it into a rustic Airbnb with an adjoining fine-dining restaurant. Unfortunately for him, the tight-knit community were vehemently opposed to the development, which stalled anyway, as the factory walls were full of asbestos.

The town also boasted a pub, which changed hands roughly every two years. Well-heeled, cashed-up couples from the city would pass through Venus Creek on sunny weekends and drop in for Sunday lunch. Over roast chicken and locally grown vegetables, one of those couples would convince themselves that they could finally quit the nine-to-five metropolitan grind and take over the lease. They would succeed where others had failed, powered by enthusiasm alone. What they didn't realise was that Venus Creek was a farming community that didn't take kindly to blow-ins, mainly because they were surplus to requirements.

City slickers were fooled into thinking their new money would revitalise an ailing town, when in fact everyone who lived in and around Venus Creek was quite wealthy. They simply eschewed ostentation. There were no gaudy mansions or Aston Martins parked in gravel driveways. The farmhouses were old weatherboard homes that had seen better days and the utes had six hundred thousand kays on the clock. Meanwhile, the land was worth tens of millions. Most residents were sitting on untouched nest eggs.

The unification of the Moore and Van der Saar dynasties had been Gattan's very own *Game of Thrones*. As Dirk van der Saar drove the Monaro to his in-laws' property, his wife looking glamorous in the passenger seat and the kids in the back, excited to visit their grandparents, he reflected upon how the Moores had been squatting on the land even longer than his Dutch ancestors. If you stood atop the hill in the paddock behind their house and surveyed the landscape, everything stretching to the horizon was theirs. Verdant, rolling pasture, dotted with the occasional herd of cattle. Bert and Angie Moore were advancing in years and had downsized their immense beef operation to three hundred head of organic, grain-fed Angus that sold for eye-watering amounts at auction. Dirk felt giddy at the prospect of inheriting a portion of the Moore fortune one day – not that he needed the money. In the meantime, his strategy was to keep Bert and Angie onside.

Consequently, Dirk never turned down an invitation to attend a Sunday barbecue at his in-laws' place. The meat and views were both spectacular, and his children were equally keen to attend. Angie allowed Alex to ride on the back of the quad bike with her. Sky stuck close to her pop-pop, who had lavished her with attention since she was little.

The driveway leading into the Moore property was in dire need of resurfacing. Rain had eroded the gravel, creating fissures that were a nightmare for vehicles with low clearance. Dirk had badgered Bert about fixing the drive, but he didn't want to spend the significant amount of money it would cost to do so. Bert preferred to carry out as much of the farm work as he could himself, which likely accounted for both his fitness and his affluence.

Dirk navigated the driveway with the utmost care. The SUV would have been a more appropriate vehicle for the visit, but he knew Bert loved seeing the Monaro in action. Bert appeared at the gate to meet them, hands raised in greeting. Dirk parked behind Jude's Mazda CX-5, of which he disapproved, but Jude was a city girl who didn't know any better. Hayley, Jude and Ebony would be joining them, at Dirk's invitation. Jude had texted him, complaining that Hayley was driving her crazy and that Ebony needed to get out of the house. He immediately asked them to come along. Despite what his daughter thought, Dirk was not a monster, and he listened, occasionally.

The kids piled out of the Monaro to hug their grandfather, and Lucy reached down to squeeze Dirk's hand. In that moment, their kids looked so young and innocent. They were lucky to still have them both.

Everyone proceeded through to the deck at the back of the homestead. It was unusual to see a Saltless family at a social gathering, but Hayley was already fussing over the food with Angie Moore, who was coeliac and sympathetic to the cause. The barbecue passed muster, the spread gleaming in the bright afternoon light, the winter sun warm and welcoming.

Jude lounged in a chair by the edge of the deck, shoes off and legs splayed, overlooking the chicken coop in the top paddock. The coop was open, and the chooks wandered the yard while Bert's dog, an enthusiastic kelpie – not that there was any other kind – called Delilah attempted to round them up. The chickens were proving uncooperative.

'What are you drinking?' Dirk asked Jude.

She glanced up at him over her sunglasses, dinnerplate Pradas that were too big for her face.

'Some zero-alcohol shit Hayley found at the IGA,' Jude said, holding up the bottle. 'Tastes like drain water.'

'You want a real beer?' Dirk asked, hefting his Esky.

'What do you have?' Jude said, checking that her wife wasn't watching. Hayley was chatting with Lucy by the barbecue.

Dirk cracked the lid of the Esky to reveal two six packs of Coopers Pale.

'Fuck, yes,' she said. 'Hand me one of those.'

Dirk gave her a bottle and she popped the top on the arm of the chair. Before Hayley could see, Jude poured the remainder of her alcohol-free beer into the garden bed, then painstakingly transferred the Coopers into the empty bottle. The froth bubbled over, and she stuck the entire rim of the bottle into her mouth to catch the overflow.

'The lengths you go to,' Dirk said.

'Mate, you have no idea,' Jude said, clinking bottles with him. 'Cheers.'

Jude Tan was the kind of lean, whip-smart, over-educated second-generation city Asian who took no prisoners and who would probably be prime minister one day. Dirk thought she was way out of Hayley's league. He'd liked her from the moment they'd met.

Alex and Ebony appeared amongst the chickens, laughing as they joined Delilah in her efforts to corral them, much to the dog's excitement. Jude and Dirk watched in silence as their kids frolicked.

'Ebony seems happy to be out and about,' Dirk said.

'Hmm,' Jude replied, savouring her contraband beer. 'She's been bizarrely circumspect of late. Like she's . . . accepted what's going to happen.'

'Not if I can help it,' Dirk said.

'You and me both,' Jude said, glancing up at him. Once again, she checked to ensure they were out of earshot. 'I appreciate it's a weird situation for you.'

'Between you and me – whatever you need, whatever it takes, I'm there, okay?'

'Everyone knows you were the donor, anyway,' Jude said. 'Worst kept secret in Gattan.'

Dirk sighed. 'Most fertile man in Gattan, too, apparently,' he said.

'Alex still seeing the shrink?' Jude asked.

'For all the good it does him,' he said, tapping his temple. 'He's broken up here. What kid wouldn't be, after what he witnessed? But what doesn't kill you makes you stronger. He'll come good, eventually.'

'He's still young,' Jude said.

'Exactly. Besides, where would any of us be without a little childhood trauma?'

'Maybe he'll write a memoir about it when he's older,' Jude suggested.

'They all will,' Dirk said, shivering at the prospect. 'There'll be a glut on the market ten years from now.'

Jude took another swig and studied Dirk, who was watching the kids with a rueful smile.

'You want to elaborate on that trauma nugget?'

'Who, me?' Dirk said, startled. He waved a hand dismissively. 'Usual stuff. The old man beat the piss out of me on the regular. Thought I was a disappointment, that I didn't have what it took to inherit the business and run it like a *real man*.'

'What's a "real man"?' Jude asked, snorting.

'Fucked if I know,' Dirk said. 'One who beats his son with a muslin sack full of oranges, apparently.'

Jude almost choked on her beer.

'Are you serious?' she said, wiping her chin.

'No bruises that way,' Dirk said, smiling faintly.

'Dude, that's horrific,' she said. 'Sorry that happened to you.'

Dirk shrugged and sipped his Coopers.

'Character building,' he said. 'Anyway, the old fuck's dead now.'

Jude nodded, absorbing the information.

'My mother was the abuser in our house,' she announced.

'She lay hands on you?' Dirk asked.

'Hands, feet, cooking implements, rakes, whatever was closest,' Jude told him. 'I used to cower under the desk in Dad's study like a trapped animal.' She grimaced at the memory.

'Your dad didn't step in?'

'He was a coward,' Jude said. 'He was scared of her, too. This is before I came out, so you can imagine her response to that bombshell.'

'The mind boggles,' Dirk said, opening another bottle. He offered one to Jude, who declined.

'Funny how we never talked about this before,' he said.

'Everything's changing,' Jude said. 'We're on the raw edge of life, now. The future's uncertain.'

'I hate to be the one to break it to you,' Dirk said, 'but it always was.'

Jude frowned. 'Feels like we didn't learn any lessons from Covid.'

'This is different.'

'Yeah, but we're still quick to turn on each other. We're destructive by nature, and, oh boy, do we love apportioning blame.'

Sky wandered into the garden, pausing beside a patch of bright orange everlasting daisies to inhale the heady scent.

'There's hope,' Dirk said. 'The future still exists.'

Jude nodded towards the three kids.

'For two of them, at least,' she said.

Abruptly, Sky picked a bunch of daisies and crushed them in her fist, scattering the petals on the grass before moving on.

'I retract my former comment,' her father said.

Jude laughed. 'Future serial killer in the making, that one.'

'CEO of a multinational company would be my preference, but I see your point,' Dirk said.

'You got plans for her to run the business one day?'

'That'll more likely be Alex,' Dirk said. 'Sky's not interested. I threw her a few shifts last summer and she only succeeded in putting customers off with her snark. She has loftier ambitions.'

'Didn't we all?' Jude said. 'What's her plan?'

'Hard to say,' Dirk told her. 'She's been into astronomy lately. I even bought her a telescope. Maybe astrophysics.'

'Could be we're looking at the first Australian woman on the moon,' Jude said.

Dirk smiled. 'It's got to be someone.'

'Lunch is ready, you two,' Lucy said, coming up behind Dirk and sliding a hand over his shoulder.

Hayley called to the children from the deck. Alex and Ebony came running, sprinting to beat each other. Alex reached the deck first, the dual advantages of age and athletic experience paying dividends. Hayley frowned when she noticed Ebony's pinched cheeks.

'What are you eating?' she said sternly.

Ebony shook her head in silent denial and began to suck frantically on whatever was in her mouth. Before she had a chance to swallow, Hayley grabbed her daughter by the hair and pinched her nose.

'Spit it out,' she said. 'Right now.'

Ebony gagged and began to choke. Every adult on the deck stopped what they were doing to stare. Bert was about to say something when Angie placed a hand on his arm and shook her head.

Ebony spat a piece of liquorice onto the wooden planks. All eyes dropped to examine the offending lolly.

Shit, Dirk thought. It was one of the Dutch treats he had managed to get Alex hooked on. Liquorice drops with a pocket of salt in the middle. An unpleasant surprise for most, but a beloved national delicacy in the Netherlands. Definitely an acquired taste. Dirk had no clue his son had brought a packet to the party. He should have gone through his pockets before they left, but he didn't think.

Hayley knew exactly what the globule sticking to the deck contained. She grew up with Dirk and had screwed her face up in disgust many times when trying them. She let out a roar of frustration and slapped Ebony across the face. The child stumbled and fell to the deck, holding her cheek, stunned.

Bert shoved past everyone and ran to the stricken child, gathering her up in his arms. He was furious.

'We don't hit kids in this house,' he said.

Hayley's eyes narrowed.

'Take your hands off my daughter,' she said. 'And don't tell me what to do. You have no idea what we're going through.'

Angie Moore placed herself between her husband and Hayley. Ebony was buried in the crook of the man's arm, bawling. Alex stood by the edge of the deck, swaying uncertainly. He knew he was to blame. His left eye twitched, as if he were about to burst into tears, too.

'Everyone calm down,' Dirk and Jude said at the same time. They glanced at each other, the corners of their mouths raising in a conspiratorial smile. Dirk moved to intercept the Moores while Jude placated Hayley. Protests were voiced. Apologies were eventually offered and accepted, but the fault lines were clear for all to see. Sky watched on from her spot in the garden, shaking her head, then she turned and walked down through the paddock towards the tiny specks of cattle in the distance. She looked up at the pale blue sky, squinting as she sought the glowing point of light that was sometimes visible during the day, despite being eight hundred and ninety million kilometres away. There it was, faint, but ever present. The planet Jupiter, god of the sky.

PART FOUR

THE YOUTHFUL COURTESAN

LONG BEFORE THE SONG OF ORPHEUS TROUBLED THE SOULS OF humanity, Jessica Barry, as she was known before she married Steve Ward, sat on a sandy embankment overlooking Windmill Creek. It was one of those interminably hot Australian summer nights, when the only relief for those by the coast came in the form of a breeze skimming in on the crests of the never-ending waves that crashed against the rocks. For those in the crowded cities, reprieve came via a cool change that swept along the concrete canyons, a brief shower conjuring petrichor, the hot, oily scent of asphalt after rain.

Jessica lounged in the heat, gazing up at the starry sky beside her closest friend, Hayley Carlisle, sounding-board for the litany of complaints, frustrations, opinions and attempts at humour that swarmed around Jess's teenage mind like a flock of colourful rosellas.

Scattered in the sand beside the girls were several empty Vodka Cruiser bottles, wild raspberry flavour. They possessed no means of playing music. This was decades before portable Bluetooth speakers. Somewhere behind them in the long grass were two pushbikes, the sole means of transport for those living their golden teenage years in the township of Gattan, unless you knew someone who not only had a licence but also had access to a parent willing to risk their car in the hands of a teenager on country roads.

The breeze and the sound of the ocean were their sole companions, apart from a white police divvy van parked on the embankment opposite. With its lights extinguished, the vehicle was virtually impossible to spot under the cover of the trees. However, the glow of Senior Sergeant Andy Stevenson's cigarette gave away his position.

'That dirty fucker's watching us,' Jess said.

'Out of which eye?' Hayley replied. 'He's half blind on his left side.'

'How do you pass the coppers entrance exam with an eye like that?'

'Must've happened after,' Hayley said.

'Surprised he's not out by the highway with his speed camera, raising revenue,' Jess said.

'Maybe he's hoping to get some pictures of us instead.'

'He thinks we can't see him,' Jess said. 'I reckon he's hoping we'll give him a show.'

'Maybe after another couple of these.' Hayley laughed, clinking bottles with her friend.

'Fuck, it's hot,' Jess said, lying back on the sand.

Hayley turned over and stretched out on her belly, hair falling over her face. 'These Cruisers make me gassy. They're too fizzy.'

'Let it rip,' Jess said.

Hayley belched loudly, making them both laugh. Jess abruptly farted, eyes widening in mock alarm. That sent them spiralling into a fit of guffawing.

'The sergeant probably heard that,' Hayley said, wiping her eyes.

'Went off like a gunshot,' Jess said, biting her lip as she tried to repeat the trick.

'Don't squeeze too hard,' Hayley warned her.

They fell into silence, sipping their drinks.

'Hey, did I tell you we won Lotto this week?' Jess said, out of the blue.

'That where you got the money for these?' Hayley asked.

'Actually, yeah,' Jess said. 'We got five numbers. Won nine hundred and seven bucks. Mum gave me a hundred and fifty of it.'

'Shit, you've been holding out on me, lottery winner,' Hayley said. 'Five, eh? That's close to the jackpot.'

'Tell me about it,' Jess said. 'One more number and we'd have won half a million. Just our luck.'

'Your dad must've lost his shit.'

'You should've seen him,' Jess said. 'Almost had a heart attack. Don't know what he'd do with the money if we did win. Piss it up the wall, probably.'

'Be wasted on him.'

'Exactly. God, he's a weirdo. Sits up all night watching old episodes of *Star Trek*, looking for continuity errors.'

'How do you mean?' Hayley asked.

'Like, he rewinds it if he sees something out of place, then writes it down in his notebook. I woke up at two this morning because someone kept shouting, "'Shields at thirty per cent, Captain!" Stormed down in my uggs and PJs and told him to turn it down. I mean, for fuck's sake, I have school in the morning.'

'It's like we're the adults and they're the kids,' Hayley said.

Jess sat up, drained her bottle and cast it aside with the others.

'Fuck it,' she said. 'Let's go for a swim.'

'We don't have any togs,' Hayley protested.

'So we go in our undies,' Jess said. 'Yours probably need a wash anyway.'

'Piss off,' Hayley said, whacking her friend on the arm. 'What about the creep across the way?'

'I have a plan to get rid of him,' Jess said, pulling her T-shirt over her head. She stood up, unzipped her shorts and ran down the embankment in her underwear. Hayley watched her go, butterflies fluttering in her belly, then finished her drink and followed suit. She plunged headlong into the creek rather than wade in slowly, being the sort of person who preferred to rip off the Band-Aid.

They swam in circles for a few minutes, luxuriating in the cool relief of the ocean channel.

'Stay here,' Jess whispered. 'I'm going to spring the trap.'

'Where are you going?' Hayley hissed. 'Jess, no.'

Jess waded to shore at the base of the embankment where the police car was parked. Under cover of darkness, she clambered up the slope and crept into the long grass. The sergeant yelped when she leapt out of the bush next to his vehicle.

'Are you whacking off in there, you sicko?' she shouted.

The senior sergeant spilt his coffee all over his lap.

'You can't be running around like that,' he sputtered. 'Put some clothes on, or I'll arrest you for indecent exposure.'

Jess struck a provocative pose.

'Or we could drop by *The Sentinel* office tomorrow morning and get them to write a story about the copper busted masturbating in front of two teenage girls,' Jess said. 'Up to you, Sergeant.'

'I wasn't . . .' Stevenson said, scowling.

'Go on, then,' Jess said, hands on her hips. 'Start your engine and fuck off.'

The policeman muttered under his breath but knew when he was beaten. He switched on the ignition, reversed the divvy van into the scrub, then sped off down the trail in a cloud of dust. Jess stood her ground, watching the tail-lights recede. Then she sprinted back through the scrub, howled a victory cry and dive-bombed into the deepest section of the creek.

* * *

MOMENTS OF HAPPINESS FOR JESSICA BARRY WERE FLEETING during that final year of high school. In a small country town like Gattan, triumphs were counted in terms of a win on the football field, a night on the beach with a group of friends and a bucket of KFC, or a frantic, fumbling orgasm in the back seat of a Holden Monaro. That was Dirk van der Saar's car, a classic he intended to restore to its former glory when he had the money.

Their destination was Outlook Beach. Dirk was in a surly mood.

'What's with you?' Jess asked.

'See for yourself,' he said, switching on the interior light and angling his head towards her, one eye still on the road in case any suicidal wombats were on the prowl. Dirk had a black eye. He winced when Jess touched the bruise. She had seen plenty like it on her mother.

'I take it that's not from footy.'

'I worked in the shop after school today,' Dirk told her.

'I thought you sold jewellery, not boxing gear.'

'I gave a customer a discount,' Dirk explained, shaking his head. 'The old man showed me the error of my ways.'

Dirk's father, Willem van der Saar, only gave away money if it served his needs. He donated to a police charity, the CFA and the RSL, not out of civic duty but to ensure they were in his debt.

'When are you going to push that old bastard down the stairs?' Jess asked.

Dirk looked at her sharply.

'He's still my dad,' he said.

'He needs to start treating you better,' Jess told him. 'Especially if he wants you to take over that business one day.'

'Told me I'd better buck up my ideas and think about the future.'

'They can't wait for us to grow up, and yet they treat us like children,' Jess said. 'People breed so they can have legal slaves.'

'Cheap labour, that's about all I am to him,' Dirk agreed.

'For now,' Jess said, stroking Dirk's hair. 'Wait until he needs you.'

Dating Dirk van der Saar was bittersweet for Jess. There was light at the end of his tunnel. His father was old and in poor health. If Dirk wanted the business it would be his, sooner rather than later. Jess's family life held no such prospect. Her parents had addiction issues and were constantly broke. If Jess didn't clean the house after school, it would be a mess. She mostly cooked her own meals. Did the shopping. Made sure the bills were paid so her family didn't wind up joining the community of swagmen eking out a meagre existence in the wetlands.

Her father used to take the occasional swipe at her when he was drunk, but he hadn't done so since Jess slashed the back of his hand with a paring knife when she was fifteen. Now her mother bore the brunt of his abuse instead. Jess wished she had a sibling to help at home. Hayley sometimes came around, but Jess didn't like the way her father leered at her. On the rare occasions Hayley stayed over, they curled up together in the same bed and locked the door.

The Monaro was the only vehicle in the car park at Outlook Beach. Jess and Dirk held hands as they walked through the dunes to a secret grassy spot, trembling with anticipation. They undressed and took their time exploring each other's bodies, a luxury unfamiliar to most their age, then they fucked until they were both sated. Afterwards, they sat naked on a blanket together, smoking Winnie Blues and looking out to sea. Dirk was always at his most tender and affectionate after they made love. It was the true version of him, Jess felt, when his guard was down, and life seemed full of possibilities.

Lights blinked on a container ship crossing the dark horizon.

'Maybe we could get jobs on a boat,' Dirk said, blowing smoke rings that floated away on the breeze. 'See the world.'

'One of those cruise ships,' Jess suggested. 'They go all over.'

Dirk nodded enthusiastically. 'I'd like to see Alaska,' he said. 'How about you?'

'South America,' Jess said. 'Brazil, Argentina, Chile. We could buy motorbikes and ride all the way down to the tip of South America, where the world ends.'

'Let's do it,' Dirk said. 'I'll sell the business once it's mine.'

'We'll leave this place and never look back.' Jess nuzzled into Dirk's neck and kissed him behind the ear. He let out a low moan and turned to kiss her on the lips. They blew smoke into each other's mouths. Jess pushed him down onto the blanket and straddled his taut stomach, holding his arms back over his head. He strained to push her off, grinning all the while, but she pinioned him effectively. The lovers emptied their heads. They didn't think about their parents, school, their tumultuous home lives, or anyone else. They existed purely in the now, focused, dreaming of a life together, ignoring that they were doomed and likely to never leave the place.

* * *

THE FINAL YEAR OF HIGH SCHOOL WAS THE MOST UNENDURABLE of Jess's life. All she wanted was to fulfil her legal obligations and walk through those doors for the final time. This was true for most students at Gattan High, few of whom harboured medical or legal career aspirations, unless you counted emptying wastepaper baskets and changing diapers on incontinent patients. Jess could hardly wait to leave school. A hairdressing apprenticeship beckoned, which had to be more interesting than interminable afternoons in Mr Harrison's English literature class. The man acted like he knew Shakespeare personally.

'Does someone have a mobile phone switched on in here?' Harrison said to his soporific class, furious at being interrupted while reading an excerpt from *The Lord of the Flies* aloud, like he was on stage at the Opera House.

'It's mine, sir,' Jess said, waving her hand. 'It's on silent, but.'

'Turn it off please, Miss Barry.'

Jess rummaged in her bag until she located the Nokia. There were eight missed calls from an unknown number. She held the power button until the screen went dark.

It wasn't until she was walking home with Hayley that she remembered to switch the phone back on. There were now fourteen missed calls. The phone buzzed in her hand.

'Who is this?' she said.

It was the receptionist at Gattan Hospital, a recent addition to the country town, courtesy of the state government. Gattan had been the cheapest site in the region. Jess listened carefully, then sighed and hung up.

'Mum's back in emergency and they can't get a hold of Dad,' Jess told Hayley. 'Probably passed out drunk in the shed and can't hear the home phone. Or he's just ignoring it.'

'I'll come with you,' Hayley said. 'It's only a fifteen-minute walk.'

Admissions was populated by the usual cross-section of elderly patients and tradies in high-vis vests holding bloodstained rags to their temples. Jess approached the receptionist, Paula, and explained why she was there.

'We've been trying to reach you all afternoon,' Paula said.

'Just finished school,' Jess told her, which should have been obvious from their uniforms. 'How is she?'

'Painkiller overdose,' Paula said matter-of-factly. 'Oxycodone. We pumped her stomach but she's still pretty out of it. Hopefully we caught it in time and there's no permanent damage.'

Hayley grimaced.

'Who brought her in?' Jess asked.

'She collapsed in the cleaning aisle at Coles,' Paula said. 'Apparently she was ranting beforehand, in a state of delirium.'

'She's had hallucinations before,' Jess said.

'She was trying to drink bleach off the shelf,' Paula told her.

Jess puffed out her cheeks, unable to process this new level of mania. 'Can we see her?'

'Not right now,' Paula said. 'The doctor wants a chat with you first. Take a seat and I'll call you when he's available.'

Hayley and Jess flipped through old issues of *Better Homes and Gardens* while they waited. Jess was not especially perturbed by the turn of events. It wasn't the first time she'd been called to the hospital; she fully expected that one day she'd be informed of the worst possible outcome.

Eventually a doctor came out of the emergency ward and scanned the waiting room. He was young, in his twenties, but not a local. He called Jess's name and she raised her hand like she was still in class. The doctor was surprised to encounter two teenage girls in school uniform.

'No guardian?' he asked.

'I'm the grown-up in the family,' Jess told him.

'I see,' the doctor said. 'I'm Doctor Ravi Mehta. Come through, please.'

The girls slouched their way into an empty treatment room and Dr Mehta closed the door behind them. There was only a single plastic chair and an examination couch. Jess hoisted herself up onto the couch, smoothing down her skirt, while Hayley flopped into the chair. Dr Mehta eyed her with suspicion.

'I don't know how much of this you want your friend to hear,' he said.

'No secrets between us,' Hayley said.

Mehta frowned in disapproval. He consulted his clipboard.

'I'm concerned about your mother's addiction to painkillers,' he told Jess.

'You and me both,' she replied.

'Her file indicates that she was prescribed Oxycodone for chronic pain, but it's worryingly light on detail.'

Jess was wise enough to make sure the story was straight. While she didn't want her mother hooked on pain meds, the cold turkey alternative held little appeal.

'She's suffered a few accidents in recent years,' she told the doctor.

'Of what nature?' he asked.

'Domestic.'

Mehta nodded knowingly and gave Jess a serious look.

'I noticed contusions on her back and torso,' he said. 'Signs of recent injury. Blunt force trauma if I had to hazard a guess. Anything you want to tell me about that?'

'It's none of your business,' Hayley interjected.

Jess held up a hand to quiet her.

'Mum's always been clumsy,' she said. 'Falls over a lot.'

'Is that so?' Mehta said. 'Problems with her coordination?'

'Yes, write that,' Jess suggested, pointing to the clipboard.

The doctor folded his arms, considering his options.

'In my experience, frequent falling is best treated by the police rather than the medical profession,' he said.

Jess felt a surge of fondness for the man. He was showing compassion, trying to help. Not something she had often witnessed in authority figures.

'That'd be a great idea if you want me to wind up in the next bed over,' Jess told him.

'You ever tried calling the cops in Gattan?' Hayley asked.

'Once, yes,' Mehta admitted. 'There was a party at the holiday house next door to us. We have a baby. I asked them to turn down the music, but their response was ... not polite. That's when I phoned the police.'

'They send a SWAT team?' Hayley asked.

Dr Mehta laughed, before letting out a deep sigh.

'I'm going to reduce your mother's Oxycodone prescription, Miss Barry, but not eliminate it entirely,' he said. 'Perhaps that will help wean her off the pills. These pain medications are highly addictive and have terrible side effects, as I'm sure you're well aware.'

'Thanks, doc, you're a legend,' Jess told him.

He handed her a pre-written script.

'A piece of advice,' he said, chewing his lip. 'I've only been in Gattan a few months, so correct me if I'm wrong, but I get the feeling this is the kind of town where marijuana is easy to source. Buy her some of that instead. And you didn't hear that from me.'

'Why, Doctor Mehta, I'm shocked,' Jess said. 'I am but an innocent eighteen-year-old schoolgirl. What would I know of illegal narcotics?'

'Nothing, I'm sure,' Mehta said, smiling. 'Any other questions while I'm here?'

'Hayley?' Jess said. 'Any gynaecological issues you'd like to discuss with Doctor Mehta?'

Hayley buried her face in her hands. When she looked up, her cheeks were crimson.

'Sorry, doctor,' she said. 'This one's incorrigible.'

Mehta took that as his cue to leave. He ushered the girls out, and they barrelled back into the admissions area, their raucous laughter curtailed by the steely glares of waiting patients. Paula promised to call Jessica when her mother was ready to be discharged. The pair walked out into the golden afternoon light.

'You got any money?' Jess asked Hayley, fanning herself with the prescription. 'I need to fill this at Chemist Warehouse.'

'Will they give it to you?'

'They have before.'

Hayley checked her wallet.

'Oh, I still have those two fifties I lifted from Mum's purse,' she said, brandishing the notes.

'Have you not spent that yet?' Jess asked, incredulous.

'Been saving it,' Hayley told her. 'Figured maybe we could go to the movies in Langdale on Saturday, if Dirk will take us.'

'He totally will,' Jess said. She checked her own wallet, pulling out a ten dollar note and several coins.

'I have enough to shout us a Whopper and a shake,' she said.

'Done deal,' Hayley said, linking arms with her friend. They crossed to the shady side of the street and began the long trek to Hungry Jack's.

* * *

JESS WAS HOPELESS AT NETBALL. SHE KEPT THINKING SHE WAS playing basketball and driving to the net. The Phys Ed teacher, Miss Jamieson, was constantly ejecting Jess for repeat offences. Jess didn't care. She preferred hockey – at least you got a stick to hit with. She enjoyed the fear on her opponents' faces when they spotted her twirling her club before a game. School was a joke to Jess. Glorified day care. A place to dump kids in the hope they might learn fractions. But the end was near, the thrill of freedom tantalisingly close.

As Jess changed into her hockey skirt, she noticed Hayley wasn't budging. She sat in the change room with her legs crossed, filing her nails. Miss Jamieson was not impressed.

'Carlisle!' she shouted. 'Why are you still in uniform?'

'Got the painters in, Miss,' Hayley said coolly.

'Is that so?' Jamieson said. There was no fooling the Phys Ed teacher. She pulled out a notepad and consulted the chart she kept of the students' menstrual cycles.

'Hmm,' Jamieson said, closing her book. 'All right, Hayley, you can watch today.' She turned to Jess, who was half-dressed in a skirt and sports bra. 'Suppose that's you out for the game too, Barry.'

'Uh, yes Miss,' Jess said, hesitantly. 'That's right.'

'See you both on the sidelines,' Jamieson said, her tone making it clear they should not attempt to hide in the library instead.

'You dill,' Hayley said as Jess changed back into her uniform.

'Joke's on her,' Jess said. 'I haven't had it yet.'

It was so punishingly hot that Jess was happy to skulk on the sidelines rather than run around red-faced while the boys on the football field craned their necks, hoping for a flash of knickers. But as the afternoon wore on, a kernel of concern formed in Jess's mind, steadily morphing into full-blown panic. After school, she raced to Chemist Warehouse and waited until someone she didn't know was on the register.

The pregnancy test confirmed what she already feared. She told no one, not even Hayley. It didn't seem real. Jess felt no different. Dirk was the father, of course. She hadn't slept with anyone else, despite what everyone thought. She imagined stalking the aisles of Woolworths with a pot belly, garnering looks of judgement. Anxiety-ridden days passed while a new life grew inside her.

After a week, Jess began to reconcile herself to the truth, realising that perhaps this wasn't such a bad thing after all. Dirk was a Van der Saar. His family were well off. A baby would strengthen their bond. They could still travel, still see the world, and then return to Gattan and settle down. In a few years' time, Dirk would be one of the wealthiest and most respected men in Gattan, whether he chose to sell the business or not. Jess's mother would soon meet an early grave at the bottom of an Oxycontin bottle and her father would likely pack up and move to a caravan park somewhere along the coast, leaving Jess alone, barely out of high school and with a baby in tow.

Dirk was her way out. They could get married, and she would live in relative ease, day-drinking with Hayley while a nanny played Legos with the child. Jessica van der Saar. It had a great ring to it. The feared matriarch, ruling Gattan with an iron fist from her mansion on Jongebloed Lane.

But ten days after the pink line, Jess was mustering the courage to break the news, first to Dirk, then Hayley, when the situation changed entirely.

She and Hayley were sitting in the shade with their backs against the bike shed, waiting for the bell to signal the end of lunch, when they overheard a group of girls from the year below discussing someone.

'He took her to Outlook Beach in his car,' one of the girls said. They were on the other side of the bike shed wall, their voices clearly audible through the wooden slats.

'They had sex on the beach,' another added, eliciting a round of gasps and giggles.

'She's lucky, he's hot,' a third voice said.

'Yeah, but so's Luce, so they're a good fit.'

'Shame about the old girlfriend,' the second girl commented.

'He's going to dump her this weekend.'

'Jess Barry?' a fourth girl said. 'She'll go off at him. She's fucking crazy.'

And that was it. The ground opened beneath her and Jess fell through into the vast unknown. Part of her wanted to smash through the slats of the bicycle shed and grab those girls by the throat, but she was overwhelmed by a sense of deflation. All she could do was hang her head between her legs and cry. Hayley consoled her friend, rubbing her back while she sobbed. She had no idea what was at stake. They did not return to class that afternoon. Hayley helped Jess home and tucked her into bed, where she wept for two days straight. Jess was broken, dreams in ruins, and all she had ahead of her was a bleak future that was kicking her in the guts.

Jess and Dirk never really broke up. Hayley let it be known that he was to leave Jess be, that she already knew he was seeing Lucy Moore, one year younger and heir to the Venus Creek dynasty. The reasons behind Dirk's actions remained obscure. Hayley whispered in her devastated friend's ear that he was just a boy, a stupid boy, led by his dick and temptation. She told Jess she had dodged a bullet, that such a man would never be faithful, that it was in his nature to betray the ones he loved. But this was cold comfort to Jess, who still harboured a secret in her womb, one that she now held a sliver of hope for.

* * *

ONE WEEK LATER, JESS WAS SPIRALLING INTO A VORTEX OF SELF-loathing. She sat slumped in a booth at McDonald's after school, staring into the middle distance, eyes glazed, poking listlessly at her strawberry sundae. Jess was alone, utterly alone, and convinced that would always be the case. Hayley was at a Bible study youth group her zealous parents insisted she attend, and Jess was lost, unmoored. She could hardly hold a thought in her head.

She had seen Dirk around, but he had pointedly ignored her. How quickly boys moved on. Jess was yesterday's news. Dirk whispered his empty promises in Lucy Moore's ear now. Jess wondered if they talked about travelling the world too, or if that had all been bluster. Her right eye twitched as she recalled how compliant she had been, how eager for his attention. As Jess's enthusiasm had been extinguished, she was left angry, and experiencing a loneliness that had hollowed out her insides.

'Excuse me, are you all right, mate?'

Jess blinked and looked up. Standing before her was a kid from Gattan High. One of the quiet guys. Cute, tousled blond hair, school tie done up in the complicated, supposedly cool knot some students were trying. Jess stared at the boy for a few seconds before she remembered his name. Steve Ward. A ruckman on the footy team but not exactly their star player.

'Not really, Steve,' Jess said. 'But what's new?'

Steve slid uninvited into the booth opposite her. Jess saw that his hands were trembling and felt a moment of sympathy. He noticed her noticing, and he gripped the edge of the table to steady his nerves.

'If you want to talk to someone,' he said, in what was obviously a huge effort, 'I'm a good listener.'

'You don't want to hear my problems,' Jess said.

'The most beautiful girl in town with the weight of the world on her shoulders?' Steve said. 'I think I do.'

Jess abruptly reached out and gripped Steve's hand. Tears streaked down her face. She couldn't stop them.

'Hey, hey,' Steve said softly, rubbing the back of her hand.

A tempest had swept through Jess's world, destroying every vestige of optimism. Two nights prior, Jess was jolted awake by cramps, the pain unlike anything she had ever experienced. She staggered into the bathroom and sat on the toilet, doubled over, grabbing her ankles and squeezing them so tightly marks were still visible days later. She knew exactly what was happening. She didn't want to look, to bear witness. She knew what she saw would be burnt forever into her brain. But she did. She had to. She sat there, sobbing quietly, until her legs went numb. And when she was certain it was over, she cleaned herself up, put a pad in her undies and curled up in bed with her trusted plushy Eeyore. *You and me against the world, buddy.* He had seen better days, but Eeyore, the cynical, depressed, misanthropic donkey, had always been there for her.

She was off the hook. No more baby, no more Dirk. Free to embrace a fresh start. And the guilt was overwhelming. Now, sitting before her, stroking her hand was the unformed and innocent Steve Ward. No longer a boy, not yet a man. He was in transition, as they all were.

'We're never finished like we often think we are, hey?' Jess asked him, body racked with sobs.

'No,' he said fiercely, pale blue eyes a beacon. 'There's always another day, another chance.'

Jess wanted to believe that more than anything. She did not want to let herself be dragged into the hell of the ordinary, the mundane. In that moment, a diamond formed deep in the centre of her chest. She would not go quietly. She would not succumb. She would fight tooth and nail for a good life. Jessica Barry would be a mother one day and when that happened, she would lavish her child with love and affection. She would hold the child tightly against her heart and never let them go.

PART FIVE

THE YOUNG APOSTATE

THE ENDLESS PASTORAL DAYS OF SUMMER, THE FIRST WEEKS OF freedom from the inconsequential high school classes, were already fading in the memory like footprints in the surf. The still, hazy afternoons spent lounging by the pool or on the beach, with nothing to do, nowhere to go, but everything to hope for. Hayley missed those days, even as she was still living in their mist. For Hayley, there was to be no summer of deep reflection and promise, no frolicking in the waves or risky romantic overtures in the dunes. Instead, Hayley was spending boundless hours with the backs of her thighs stuck to an uncomfortable wooden pew, bored out of her mind. She'd resorted to flipping through the hymn book, calculating how old the white male lyricists were when they shuffled off. Their years of birth and death were conveniently listed in the Gattan Anglican Church hymnal – by some indifferent soul, Hayley presumed, who had suffered through her exact predicament.

The new pastor, Ian Monroe, was disarming. He was a 26-year-old from the city with a Scottish burr, black-rimmed glasses and Converse sneakers. At first, Hayley had high hopes for this young man who was stepping in while their regular minister was on sabbatical. Sadly, these hopes were dashed the moment the Scotsman opened his mouth, letting loose a brand of vile invective that may have pleased the elderly parishioners, who believed gay people sprang fully formed from the ground in the 1980s, but to Hayley's conflicted ears made him sound like a Nazi Ewan McGregor.

'Homosexuality is a personality disorder that promotes dangerous sexual addictions and aggressive, anti-social impulses,' Monroe said, to much nodding of heads. 'The gay and lesbian movement is evil. Their goal is to defeat Christian society and replace it with a culture of sexual promiscuity. Homosexuals have turned away from worshipping the true and living God and his transcendent moral order, choosing instead to worship a false idol of chaos. Their lifestyle carries enormous physical and mental health risks, not least of which is the corruption of innocent children. They would teach them from a young age that their deviant lifestyle is perfectly natural, causing our youth to develop into adults who are desensitised to this harmful immorality.'

That was a lot to take in for a young woman who had spent an inordinate amount of time internalising the desires and attractions she had experienced throughout her young life. Hayley looked around at the familiar faces in the congregation. Most of those present had known her since she was a child. She understood that they'd grown up in different times, and that hatred of those who were different was perhaps like fine wine, becoming more piquant and exacting with age. Still. Times were changing, whether her mother, father and their church friends liked it or not. Same-sex marriage had been legalised in the Netherlands and Belgium. Other countries seemed certain to follow suit, although in Australia such freedom remained a distant, unlikely prospect.

In the meantime, Hayley could only wait, and hide, and try not to give herself away. Gattan was a small rural community. Coming out would be akin to painting a target on her back. Hayley had learnt from an early age that she needed to be a master of disguise, a mistress of subterfuge. It was exhausting pretending to be someone else all the time, especially while still trying to work out who you really were. Hayley's feelings alternated often: confusion, certainty, fear, hope and depression were all on her emotion merry-go-round. Most of the time she was simply frazzled, appearing composed while secretly on the verge of a breakdown.

Having completed his diatribe against perversion, Pastor Monroe chose a modern hymn, written by Ruth C. Duck in 1987. What a stellar year for hits, Hayley mused. 'Wash, O God, our Sons and Daughters' was right up there with Kylie Minogue's 'Locomotion'.

Hayley pulled her usual trick of singing the melody half a beat behind everyone else so that when the congregation reached the end of the hymn and fell silent, Hayley's final, squeaky, 'God transform!' echoed around the hall in isolation.

Her mother elbowed her painfully in the ribs.

'Keep up,' she hissed.

At the end of the service, the pastor made a beeline for Hayley. Eager proselytisers could always sense a lost soul in need of guidance, or at the very least, behavioural correction.

'Your mother informs me you've been listening to questionable music, Hayley,' Monroe said.

'Eminem's new album,' Hayley declared. 'It's hardly devil worship, pastor.'

Monroe frowned and pressed the bridge of his glasses.

'I'm not sure Fifty Cent and his friends are ideal Christian role models,' he said.

The pastor thought he was down with the kids.

'It's Fiddy,' Hayley told him.

'Whatever he calls himself, please be careful and don't pay close attention to their message,' Monroe pleaded.

'You're probably right,' Hayley said. 'I've been thinking of experimenting with more wholesome country music, like k.d. lang.'

Monroe choked briefly then cleared his throat.

'Yes, well, perhaps further research is required before proceeding,' he said.

'Preach,' Hayley said, making a sideways pistol with her forefinger and thumb like they did in rap videos. Monroe looked confused for a second, unsure if this was an appropriate gesture in the hallowed confines of a church.

Hayley's mother berated her on the drive home.

'I don't know why you can't behave in church,' she said.

'Because I don't want to be there,' Hayley said. Lately, she had been trying open defiance on for size.

'That Jessica Barry is a bad influence on you,' her mother said.

Of that, Hayley had no doubt, but she enjoyed Jess's influence. Later that same day, Hayley climbed out her bedroom window while her parents were watching television and crossed Gattan armed with a backpack containing a torch, a plastic bottle of fake blood, a towel, an old bikini she didn't wear anymore and the Polaroid camera she'd received for her eighteenth birthday. Jess was waiting for her on the corner of Watt Street.

'You get away all right?' Jess asked.

'Yeah, Mum and Dad were camped out in front of *Antiques Roadshow*,' Hayley said nervously. 'Even the Rapture couldn't drag them away. Mum would ask the Four Horsemen of the Apocalypse if they wouldn't mind waiting twenty minutes. Pestilence would be like, ooh, *Antiques Roadshow*, I've got a tapestry I'd love them to look at.'

'Too many religious references for me, mate,' Jess said.

'Sorry, I was dragged to morning services today.'

'Again? They're going, like, four times a week,' Jess said. 'They do know it's summer break, right?'

'That's why,' Hayley said. 'They don't want me getting into trouble.'

'They banned you from seeing me yet?'

'Pretty much.'

The girls assessed their target. It was early evening in Gattan, and the streets were quiet. The heat of the day had dissipated; most residents were probably either sitting by the barbecue in their backyard or crowding onto one of the local beaches. There was a night market in Sandy Bay, twenty kilometres along the coast. The perfect time for a spot of larceny.

The previous incarnation of Gattan High was fenced off, all the windows boarded up. The school had closed five years earlier, and the promised redevelopment had never happened. Now, the building lay derelict. Signs on the wire fence claimed the premises were patrolled by security, but everyone knew that wasn't true. The council wanted to convert the building into a creative space, but there were no takers, and with each passing year the grounds presented more of a challenge to prospective buyers. Grass sprouted through cracks in the concrete. The basketball court was a tangle of weeds. Someone had tried to burn the place down once, leaving a black scar against the north wall. The lawns were badly overgrown, and possibly home to copperhead snakes.

While Hayley kept watch, Jess prised a plank away from a ground-floor window using a crowbar she'd pinched from her dad's shed. Once the gap was wide enough, she threw her backpack in first and then squeezed through after it. Hayley did the same, stepping down into the classroom. It reeked of stale urine.

They illuminated their torches and cast the beams around the room. A stack of chairs had fallen, scattering wooden seats across the floor. Desks were pushed up against the wall, and the parquetry was cracked and broken. Some wag had scrawled, 'Darwin was right' on the blackboard, alongside the slightly less philosophical, 'Go Tigers'.

'You think anyone's squatting in here?' Hayley asked, her stomach churning.

'Nah,' Jess said. 'I checked around before you arrived. All locked down tight. Jeez, it stinks, but.'

The walls of the corridor were covered in tags. Broken glass crunched underfoot. Jess led the way, mounting the stairs to the first floor. These rooms were not as damaged. Halfway down the corridor on the left, they found a bathroom that was relatively unmolested. The door hung askew but at least the stalls didn't stink and the large mirror over the sinks was mostly intact. Detritus littered the floor, but Hayley and Jess managed to sweep most of it out of the way with their feet.

'Good spot, you reckon?' Jess asked.

'Perfect,' Hayley agreed, leaning over one of the sinks to scrutinise her face in the mirror. A beam of light crossed the bathroom, coming from a broken window high on the back wall. Jess produced half-a-dozen tealight candles from her pack and lit them, placing them judiciously around the room for extra light.

Hayley set the bottle of fake blood and camera on the counter between the sinks, then picked up the Polaroid.

'Quick snap before we begin?' she asked.

'Sure.' Jess threw an arm around Hayley's shoulder and grinned louchely at the mirror. Hayley took the photo, acutely aware of the smell of Jess's hair as they tilted their heads together. The camera whirred, spitting out a white rectangle. Instead of shaking it, Hayley held the photograph to her chest.

'Heat develops them faster,' she explained.

'I'm going to get changed,' Jess said.

'Maybe we should do that in the corridor and leave our clothes out there, so we don't get paint on them?' Hayley suggested.

'Smart,' Jess said, grabbing her pack and stepping out of the bathroom. Hayley took a deep breath before following her.

She had never felt so nervous. Jess was inscrutable. It was difficult to gauge her mood.

They stripped in the corridor and, for the briefest of moments, stood naked together in the abandoned building. Hayley didn't know where to look; her eyes were inexorably drawn towards Jess's lithe form. She had seen her friend in the buff many times before, at the beach and in the communal showers at school, but this was different. This had an edge that made Hayley tremble so hard her teeth began to chatter.

'You cold?' Jess asked as she pulled up her bikini bottoms.

'Yeah, it's not that warm in here, eh?' Hayley lied.

They both laughed nervously.

'This is so weird,' Jess said. 'Come on, let's stage a murder.'

The two girls padded gingerly back into the bathroom. Jess opened the bottle of fake blood and began squirting it around the room.

'Spatter some across the mirror,' Hayley suggested. 'Like an arterial spurt.'

'You're an arterial spurt,' Jess said, turning the bottle on her friend, who shrieked as Jess sprayed her with sticky red goo.

'Hey, I'm meant to be the crime scene photographer, not the victim,' Hayley squealed.

'All right, do me,' Jess said, handing her the bottle.

Jess stood, arms wide, back arched, eyes closed, waiting. Hayley tried to swallow but her throat was dry. Covering her bikini-clad friend in red paint was the most erotic act in which she had ever engaged. A voice in her head kept telling her to calm down, this was nothing, just a bit of fun, don't spoil it.

Once Jess was smothered in blood, she turned to look at herself in the mirror and laughed maniacally.

'Fucking awesome,' she said. 'Get some photos.'

Hayley wiped her hands on the towel and began taking photographs. Jess adopted a variety of dramatic poses before lying on the ground and playing dead. Hayley quickly squirted the last of the fake blood on the wall behind her and in a pool on the floor next to Jess's hips.

'Let your hair fall across your face,' she directed. 'One knee up against the wall, then open your legs a bit.'

'Perve,' Jess said, spitting out fake blood. 'This stuff tastes like shit.'

'It's just syrup with food dye,' Hayley said. 'Won't do you any harm if you swallow it.'

'That's what all the boys say.'

Hayley kept shooting until she ran out of film. As she was getting up, Jess slipped and almost cracked her head on the sink. Hayley helped her to her feet, laughing. They stood next to each other, facing the mirror again.

'Like a horror movie,' Jess said. 'I love it.'

She put her arm around Hayley and leant into her shoulder, then moved behind her, wrapping her arms around Hayley's torso to warm her up. The sensation of Jess's hands gliding across her skin sent a shiver through the entire length of Hayley's body. She yearned to lean back into Jess's neck, but she was terrified to do so. In the end, Jess planted a gentle, chaste kiss on Hayley's collarbone.

'Thanks for doing this, mate,' she said. 'I really needed it. You're the best.'

An ocean roiled within Hayley. She knew Jess was devastated about Dirk. She wanted to console her friend, wanted to tell her how she felt about everything, about her. But she was so afraid of ruining their friendship, of revealing it to be a veneer. The risk was too great.

Hayley had been finding lately that there were moments when time seemed to stand still. And here she was, the road before her branching in two directions. She could wait by the crossroads, filled with regret. Or . . . fifty-fifty. Win or lose.

Hayley turned to face Jess and pulled her close. She was taking the gamble. Her trembling lips parted, and she kissed her friend on the mouth. Jess's entire body tensed, and her neck snapped back as she pulled away.

'What the fuck are you doing?'

'Sorry, just, you know,' Hayley said weakly.

They let go of each other and Jess retreated, frowning.

'Yeah, nah,' she said.

'Totally,' Hayley said. 'Sorry, don't know why I did that. Thought it would be funny. Just forget it.'

Jess regarded her dubiously. 'You need to get out more,' she said.

'You're not wrong.' Hayley turned back to the sink so she wouldn't have to face the disapproval on Jess's face. Desperate to change the subject, she fiddled with the taps. The pipes groaned.

'Shit, there's no water,' Hayley said. 'How are we going to get cleaned up?'

Jess stepped over to the next sink, looking sideways at her friend, brow furrowed as if considering something for the first time.

'I'd say wipe me down with the towel, but I'm not sure I can trust you,' Jess said.

'Don't be stupid.' Hayley dismissed her friend's concern with a wave of her bloody hand, smiling ruefully. 'You're not my type, anyway.'

Jess snorted, still unsure. They stood side by side in silence for a moment, gazing at each other's blood-streaked reflections.

* * *

HAYLEY DIDN'T NORMALLY AGREE TO DAY TRIPS IN THE CAR WITH her parents, mainly because reading in the car made her nauseated, and the queasy hours would drag like a blunt Lady Gillette across a stubbled shin. In addition, her parents listened to Christian radio stations, soft rock sung by earnest men with mullets, featuring lyrics about being high on the Lord. It never ceased to amaze Hayley how many rhymes those songwriters found for the word 'holy'. She presumed the first order of business when forming a Christian rock band was to invest in a decent thesaurus.

However, she was willing to make an exception to visit Rushglen, a tiny town nestled in the hills behind Venus Creek. The road to Rushglen boasted spectacular views over the farmland surrounding Gattan, as well as the occasional precipitous drop into a gorge. The town had twelve houses and a derelict service station with a faded Shell logo. If it weren't for the Saturday market, no one would ever go there.

The market featured retro furniture, records, handmade clothes, candles, crystals, locally grown organic fruits and vegetables, vegan samosas, second-hand books, chopping boards carved from fallen trees, and a decent cup of chai. These goods were traded by hirsute, dreadlocked, barefooted, environmentally conscious stall holders who flocked to the town from across the region. Hayley loved it. Even her conservative parents approved. Her mother could happily while away an hour in the bush garden, chatting about native plants while her dad scoured the stalls looking for knick-knacks.

They parked on the verge a hundred metres from the market. They dropped three gold coins into a bucket at the entry and were welcomed by an elderly man with a white beard down to his navel, who was playing a fiddle. Hayley's dad disappeared into the main shed, where grizzled hills-dwellers had laid out their wares for inspection. Hayley fell into step behind her mum, who marched straight to the cake stand. She inspected the treats on offer.

'Are these made using refined sugar or honey?' Hayley asked the woman behind the counter, who raised an eyebrow in appreciation of the question.

'If you're looking to avoid processed sugars, try one of the mellow balls,' she said.

'One of those and a soy chai latte, please.'

Hayley's mother gave her a disapproving look but forked over the cash. There was no EFTPOS at the Rushglen market. That would mean declaring income to the ATO.

Mother and daughter found a table in the shade to enjoy their morning tea. Hayley's mum had a pot of Earl Grey and a lemon slice.

'Fully loaded,' Hayley pointed out. 'Dairy, gluten, sugar, the works.'

'How's your mellow ball?' her mum asked sceptically.

'Delicious,' Hayley said, taking a bite. She sniffed the coconutty treat. 'I think it might have marijuana in it.'

Penny Carlisle almost choked on her Earl Grey.

'I'm kidding,' Hayley said, although she wasn't. The mellow ball had a definite whiff about it, and the name was a dead giveaway.

'Why don't you want to eat sugar?' her mother asked.

'Rots the organs,' Hayley told her. 'I read about it online. Too much glucose leads to kidney damage.'

'You mean diabetes,' Penny said. 'You're a few decades away from having to worry about that.'

'Best to start healthy eating habits early, don't you think?' Hayley asked. 'Imagine how much sugar you've consumed in your lifetime, Mum. Must be thousands of kilos.'

'I burn it off.'

'How?'

'By keeping fit,' Penny said, devouring another spoonful of lemon slice.

'I've never seen you exercising,' Hayley said.

'I shift from one foot to the other when I'm standing at the sink.'

'Mum, that's not a workout,' Hayley said. 'That's called standing.'

'I'm always picking up after you,' Penny said haughtily. 'Hence my bad back.'

'No, you have spinal pain because you don't do enough physical activity.'

'How come you're such an expert in everything?'

'How come you're not?' Hayley said, exasperated. 'You're thirty years older than me. You'd think you'd have worked out by now that sitting on your arse all day munching Arnott's biscuits is bad for your health.'

'I'll wash that mouth out with soap if you're not careful, young lady.'

'This is the twenty-first century, Mum,' Hayley told her.

'Are you implying that I'm old-fashioned? Excuse me for espousing traditional family values.'

Hayley glanced at the pansexual hippies manning the stalls in Rushglen market, sensing an opportunity for gentle exploration.

'Our church is stuck in the past, Mum,' she said. 'The definition of family is expanding, and we're not moving with the times.'

Her mother arched an eyebrow. 'You need to sit down with Pastor Monroe for a stern talk,' she said. 'Where are you getting these heretical notions?'

'Heretical?' Hayley said, laughing. 'Really, Mum? What, so anyone with an opinion contrary to church dogma is a witch? What will the pastor do, have me burnt at the stake? Dunked in the creek to drown me and prove my innocence?'

'Sounds like you need a full exorcism,' Penny muttered. She was joking – or maybe she wasn't.

Hayley popped the last of the mellow ball into her mouth and left her mother to her early onset diabetes. She browsed the stalls, trying on a few tops she couldn't afford. A young woman offered to balance Hayley's chakras, but she felt no different after. The woman recommended a kinesiology session so Hayley could confront the deep-seated trauma she was carrying in her sacrum.

She took the woman's business card and promised to call, having no intention of doing so. The stranger pressed a clutch of leaflets into Hayley's hands, urging her to educate herself about what was really going on in the world.

Hayley discarded most of the pamphlets but kept one about the Socialist Alliance, partly because she knew it would irritate her parents but also because she was genuinely intrigued by their agenda.

The Carlisle family left the market an hour later, when an impromptu performance of 'Across the Universe' began in the garden, on guitar accompanied by bongos. Hayley's parents did not approve of The Beatles. They were devil worshippers, as evidenced when their records were played backwards.

Despite the risk of motion sickness, Hayley could not resist the urge to read aloud from the political tract as they drove back down the narrow mountain road.

'The SA are campaigning for eco-socialist changes that will transform society and the economy,' she said.

'What on earth are you babbling about?' her mother said.

Hayley held up the pamphlet. 'The Socialist Alliance. Radical democracy and progressive social change giving voice to the exploited and oppressed. I'm thinking of joining.'

'Don't talk nonsense,' Penny said.

Hayley barrelled ahead, aware of the sudden increase in her heart rate.

'More rights for women and asylum seekers,' she said. 'An end to religious exemptions for discrimination against the gay and lesbian community.'

'That's enough, Hayley,' her father said, his voice a low growl. His wife glanced at him, startled. She rarely saw him angry.

'I don't get it,' Hayley said. 'Why would you be opposed to equal rights?'

'We're not,' Penny said hesitantly. 'Those poor boat people should be treated humanely. It's a disgrace how we shun them. We're all God's children.'

'You care more for them than your own daughter,' Hayley said.

'Don't be ridiculous,' Penny said, shaking her head as if she didn't want to hear another word.

'You can't have a preference when it comes to oppressed peoples,' Hayley pressed ahead. 'For a true Christian, it's all or nothing.'

'Hayley, can you stop now, please?' her mum said. 'I've just about had enough.'

Hayley's stomach flipped. This was another one of those crossroad moments, and she was tired of standing still, eyes cast to the ground.

'Just out of interest,' she said, steeling herself, 'what if one of the letters in that acronym that scares you so much applied to your daughter?'

Silence reigned inside the vehicle. A magpie swooped across the road, narrowly missing the windscreen.

'The "L", say,' Hayley added.

Her father leant back and snatched the pamphlet from Hayley's unsuspecting fingers, momentarily taking his eyes off the road.

'I said, that's *enough*!' he shouted, much too loudly in the small space.

'Dad!' Hayley screamed and inhaled sharply.

The road that snaked through the hills from Rushglen left no margin for error. When Joe Carlisle turned back to the road, he was met with the sight of a Harley-Davidson struggling to navigate the bend. The motorcycle was close to the centre line, which Joe's Honda Civic was already straddling.

Joe clutched the steering wheel, braked hard and tried to manoeuvre his family out of trouble. The biker leant in as far as he could, the end of his handlebar striking the Honda's wing mirror as the two vehicles scraped past each other. The Harley wobbled, but its rider managed to remain upright. The Honda, however, ran out of road. Its back wheels skidded on the loose gravel on the verge and the rear of the car slewed around. Hayley had the presence of mind to lock her arms across her chest like she was dive-bombing into the creek. Just then the car fishtailed off the edge of the road, plummeting into the void.

As the front end of the car tipped and struck a huge tree branch, the windscreen shattered. Glass shards blew through the interior like a hurricane. Joe hung grimly onto the steering wheel while Penny's arms flailed like an inflatable wind dancer. The car plummeted through the bush, striking rocks and trees as it fell. Airbags deployed, cushioning the impact for Hayley's parents. As they tumbled thirty metres through nothing, a macabre thought occurred to Hayley: that her dad would rather drive off a cliff than face the humiliation of having a queer daughter.

There was no airbag in the back to protect Hayley. When the car sideswiped a gum tree, she bit off a piece of her tongue. Her seatbelt held firm, and as the bottom of the gully approached, for a nanosecond she thought the worst might be over. But then the crumpled vehicle hit a tree stump and she was flung sideways. Her temple smacked against the rear passenger window, the glass fractured in her face, and everything went black.

* * *

HAYLEY WAS SWINGING ON A ROPE SUSPENDED FROM A STORM cloud. She couldn't tell what the rope was attached to, but she clung to it with all her strength, knowing that if she let go, the fall would last forever. The pendulous arc of the swing carried her through the cloud into clear air. A vast cityscape lay below; she was headed straight for it. Skyscrapers loomed on all sides, and Hayley knew it would be tricky navigating those glass canyons. As the structures reached out for her, her knuckles turned white. She was going to hit the Westpac building; there was no way to avoid the impact. *This is it*, she thought, with rising panic. *This is how it ends. Killed by a major bank.*

Her eyes opened and she took a deep, ragged breath. Then the pain came, and her vision went fuzzy for several agonising seconds before clearing.

Hayley blinked and looked around. She was in a hospital. Much too nice for Gattan. She was on a ward with five other beds. Two were empty, but three contained sleeping patients. There were fresh flowers in a vase on her bedside table and her phone was there too, considerately plugged into a charger.

She tried to sit up and immediately regretted it. A heavy bass beat pounded in her head. She reached a trembling hand up to her temple to discover a bandage wrapped around her skull and a section of hair missing. Trying not to panic, she took a rapid inventory of her body parts. Arms, legs, fingers and toes were all intact. Sensing an unfamiliar discomfort, she peered under the sheet and discovered that she was wearing a nappy, and that she had recently pissed herself. Two of her fingers were in plaster. The sharp pain when she twisted suggested a couple of ribs might be fractured, but otherwise she was relatively unscathed. *Must have bounced right off the building*, she thought. She tentatively touched her face with her uninjured hand and decided it was probably good there were no mirrors in the vicinity. There were a multitude of tiny dressings on her face and a brief flashback reminded her of the glass exploding as she shut her eyes.

So much for my modelling career, she mused. Still, at least she was alive. She felt woozy and winced at the jackhammer pulse in her temple, reminding herself she'd had worse hangovers after drinking too much rum and Red Bull.

She lay back on the pillow and faded once more into unconsciousness. When she woke, it was daytime, and a nurse came in to help remove the nappy and clean her up.

'Any chance of some regular undies?' she croaked.

The nurse beamed.

'We can arrange that,' she said. 'Promise me you won't try walking to the bathroom unassisted. Not yet at least.'

Hayley fought back against the feeling of terror that threatened to engulf her. As was often the case when frightened, she resorted to inappropriate humour. 'Give it to me straight,' she said. 'Will I be able to play the violin again?'

'Only if you could before,' the nurse said.

'You've already heard that one,' Hayley said. 'Sorry, I don't have much in the way of bedridden post-accident material.'

'At least you're not brain damaged,' the nurse said.

Hayley's eyes widened in alarm. 'Are you sure? It's been up for debate in the past.'

'The MRI was clear,' she said. 'Do you remember what happened?'

Her head smashing through a window. Feeling like she was going to die. She swallowed and shook it off. She had a metallic taste in her mouth. 'I remember being trained to kill in a variety of ways, and that my real name is Charlene Baltimore,' Hayley said. 'Wait, am I a sleeper CIA agent?'

'No, that's the plot to *A Long Kiss Goodnight*,' the nurse said.

'I thought it sounded familiar,' Hayley said, coughing then wincing with the pain. 'Big Geena Davis fan.'

'Maybe we'll put it on later,' the nurse said, indicating the television screwed to the wall.

Hayley nodded towards the only bed with a drawn privacy curtain.

'More serious than me?' she asked.

'Same same. You'll meet her when she comes out of sedation. Keep an eye on her for me, will you?'

Hayley took a beat. 'Are my parents still alive?'

The nurse nodded. 'They're both in Gattan Area Hospital.'

Relief, tinged with regret and a healthy dose of guilt. 'We call it GAH,' Hayley told her.

The nurse smirked. 'Your dad has a broken jaw and can't talk. Your mum fractured her clavicle and is in some discomfort, but they'll be okay. We'll let them know you're out of danger.'

'Like they'll care,' Hayley said. That was rough. Uncalled for. Of course they'd care. Wouldn't they?

The nurse stared at her knowingly.

'The doctor wants to keep you here for a week's observation,' she said. 'We need to monitor for potential blood clots on the brain and the manifestation of assassin abilities.'

'Gotcha,' Hayley said, content she was in good hands. She could relax, sort of. 'So, if I feel the need to bleach my hair white, apply lipstick and stab a porter with a scalpel during my escape, I should press the buzzer and let you know?'

'We understand you may not want your former boss at the CIA to catch up with you, but, yes, please try to avoid stabbing the porters.'

In the days that followed, boredom reigned supreme. Hayley endured the humiliation of a bedpan for forty-eight hours before demanding the right to shuffle to the bathroom on her baby deer legs. She also managed to take a shower while a nurse remained nearby in case of collapse. She went weak at the knees the first time she spied herself naked in the bathroom mirror. Black, blue and scratched up, her body was an ordnance survey map of bruises and cuts. The nurse had to help her into a fresh pair of pyjamas after applying antiseptic creams, balms and fresh dressings to the wounds. Hayley swallowed a suite of pills several times a day to dull the pain. She spent most of her time dozing.

The phone call with her mother was curt; Penny's tone was muted. Hayley couldn't work out if she blamed her daughter for the accident or if it was the result of heavy medication. They reassured each other that all was well, given the circumstances, and that they would reunite once discharged. The prospect of being back home with her parents held little appeal for Hayley, who was enjoying what amounted to a free mini break in the city, complete with drugs and movies.

A card and a box of Cadbury Favourites (Party Edition) arrived from Pastor Monroe, who reminded Hayley that God was watching over her. She was yet to see any evidence of His presence.

Jess texted constantly. She was waiting until visitors were permitted, although already dreading the long trip to the city.

On day three, Hayley awoke to discover the privacy curtain around the bed across the way had been pulled back. The patient was sitting up, propped against two pillows. Her arms were folded across her chest. She looked disgruntled.

'What time's breakfast in this joint?' she asked.

Hayley gingerly wiped sleep from her eyes. Her face was still swollen.

'Soon, but don't get your hopes up,' Hayley told her. 'I thought you were under heavy sedation.'

The girl glanced around. 'Guess they removed all the sharp objects,' she said.

'You'll have to excuse this,' Hayley said, indicating her dishevelled, bruised, swollen body. 'I'm trying a new look. Medical goth near-death chic.'

'Ha,' the girl said. 'You look like you've been stitched together from dead bodies.'

'Yeah, I'm seventy per cent certain these legs aren't mine,' Hayley said, pulling up her pyjama bottoms to show off her bruised pins. 'I don't remember having such sturdy thighs.'

'I only have these,' the girl said, holding up her bandaged wrists.

'Cool,' Hayley said, instantly regretting it. 'Hey, I have some chocolates here, if you want a little pre-breakfast sugar hit.'

'Totally, chuck one over,' she said. 'I'm Jude, by the way.'

'Hayley. You want a Chomp or a Freddo?'

'No Caramello Koalas?' Jude asked.

'Nah, I ate those first.'

'Chomp me, then,' Jude said.

'My arms are too sore to throw,' Hayley said. 'I'll bring you the box.'

She swung her legs out of the bed and staggered across the ward.

'Shift over,' she said, levering herself up onto the edge of the bed and handing Jude the box of chocolates. She rummaged through them, claiming the remaining Chomp bars.

'What's your story?' Jude said, groaning in pleasure as she bit into the chocolate.

'Car crash,' Hayley said. 'Kinda my fault.'

'How so?' Jude asked.

The debate in Hayley's mind over whether to tell this stranger the truth was brief. In between naps, she'd already been hatching plans to leave Gattan and move into a share house in the city. Maybe get a job or apply for a course. She had nothing left to lose.

'I almost came out to my religious parents,' Hayley said, hardly able to believe she had spoken the words aloud.

'Almost?' Jude said, raising an eyebrow.

'I got as far as "L".'

Jude cackled in amusement. 'Oh well, that's one more letter than I've managed,' she said. 'My mum would disown me if she knew.'

The sun broke the horizon at the base of Hayley's spine, warmth curling along her vertebrae and filling her head with blinding light. *I knew it*, she thought triumphantly. *I fucking knew it.* Her parents and basically everyone in Gattan would turn their backs on her, but there were millions of people in the world who would simply shrug and move on, no big deal.

'I'm still exploring, of course,' Hayley added hastily, not wanting Jude to think she was coming on to her.

'Sure, that's the fun part,' Jude replied. 'Hey, if anyone's giving you a hard time, tell them to go fuck themselves. And if you can't do that, send them to me and I'll do it for you.'

'Is that some gay code of honour I should be aware of?'

'No, I just like shouting at people.'

From then on, the tedium of the ward was tempered by the friendship that blossomed between them. Jude was cynical in a similar manner to Jess, except her outlook was more worldly, and she was nowhere near as caught up in herself. Jude and Hayley talked about travelling across Thailand on buses, about seeing the Northern Lights, about books and comics they loved, and movies they loathed. They circled each other warily yet buoyed with delight, surprised by their instant connection and amused by the circumstances under which they met. Romance was so obviously on the cards and yet still they danced, prolonging those early days of getting to know each other, of making each other laugh, of forming a bond that felt right.

They shared their first tentative kiss on a fire escape, after sneaking off the ward one night. *Don't fall in love, don't fall in love,* Hayley told herself when she slipped back into bed. Was it already too late? There was no way of knowing the exact moment her life changed, but in later years Hayley would recall that warm night on the fire escape, the sounds of city traffic rising from below, the neon lights of the advertising hoarding on the building opposite and think, *yes, that was it, that was when I accepted my true self.*

Jess's visit, when it came, was brief and predictable. Jessica Barry was no fool. Once the small talk was over, she looked at Hayley and Jude together and immediately understood what was happening.

'I was going to tell you something but now I'm thinking, why bother?' she said.

'Go on, then,' Hayley urged her. 'You've already decided you know everything about me, apparently. Might as well get it off your chest.'

Jess cast her steely gaze across Hayley and Jude, sizing them up with disdain.

'Nah,' she said, as if turning a key over her heart. 'It cost me twenty-six bucks to get here, you know, and it took four hours.'

'Do you want a refund?' Jude scoffed.

Jess glared at her.

'Next time, try cutting along the vein, mate, rather than across,' she said.

Jude was out of bed in a flash. Hayley stepped between them, reaching down to clasp Jude's hand in hers. Jess noticed the choice she'd made and nodded.

'That's that, then,' she said. 'See you around, Carlisle.'

With that, Jess turned on her heel and marched out of the hospital.

'She'll come around,' Jude reassured Hayley, who, despite the nature of the confrontation, was upset at losing her friend over something so innocuous and commonplace as romantic entanglement.

'I wouldn't bet on it.'

PART SIX

PART SIX

HEIR TO THE THRONE

THE FLEETING PROMISE OF SUMMER DISSIPATED INTO THE implacable reality of autumn, and the best laid plans of Gattan's youth amounted to naught. Jessica withdrew from her friendship circle and threw herself into a hairdressing apprenticeship, avoiding contact with anyone she disliked, which was pretty much everyone. Hayley returned home from hospital and passed the indolent summer days recovering from her injuries in the same house as her recalcitrant, resentful parents, who had their own problems to contend with. Hayley's father hardly spoke to her all summer, and she was sure that wasn't only because of his fractured jaw. Hayley waited patiently, biding her time until she could leave.

Dirk van der Saar spent that hot, hazy summer begrudgingly toiling in his father's jewellery store, earning minimum wage. Away from the routine and structure of school, Dirk felt adrift. As possibility was supplanted by uncertainty, he found the freedom to be overwhelming. And soon he discovered its footnote, the asterisk he had previously failed to notice: *Money required.*

He broke the monotony by playing football, which should, in theory, have restored some of his wounded pride. The reality of the regional competition soon brought him down to earth.

As Dirk leapt to take his first mark of the new season, a bony fist corkscrewed into his left kidney. Dirk went to ground, rolling over in pain but still holding on to the ball. The whistle blew. The opposition player towered over him. The man spat in Dirk's face, then spun and jogged away. Dirk wiped the spittle from his cheek as he stood, swearing at the disappearing player.

'Language,' the umpire said.

'He spat on me,' Dirk complained.

'You're not in high school anymore, son.'

One of Dirk's teammates barged into him.

'Kick the fucking goal and shut up,' he said.

Dirk spun the football in his hands as he stalked backwards. He took a short run-up and drop-punted the ball towards the posts. It should have been an easy six points, but the ball struck an upright and bounced out for a behind.

The same player charged into Dirk from behind, knocking him to the ground. Dirk leapt to his feet immediately and grabbed the man's guernsey. They tussled for a moment before Dirk was hit by a second player. He tumbled sideways and felt a twinge in his knee before crumpling on the grass, the earth still hard and jagged after a summer of relentless heat.

'Fucking idiot,' someone said as they ran past. Dirk felt a sharp pain as boot studs pressed into his knuckles. He gathered himself up and limped to the sideline. The exasperated coach subbed him out and Dirk slumped to the grass, rubbing his hand and knee. He sat there for the rest of the quarter.

'I'm putting you back in on the next rotation,' the coach told him as players streamed from the field.

'My knee and hand are fucked,' Dirk protested.

'Suck it up, princess,' the coach said.

Dirk sprayed Deep Heat on his injuries and hobbled through the final quarter of the game. His fellow players made a point of not passing to him if they could help it. At the final siren, he was jostled and barged all the way to the showers. The Gattan Crows lost to the Kingtown Warriors by fifty-three points. As Dirk was getting dressed, the coach approached him.

'If you can't handle a little sledging, you're not going to last in this league,' he said. 'You may be used to kicking six goals a game without breaking a sweat for Gattan High, but you're playing with men now.'

Dirk glanced around the change room. There were no friendly faces, no arms around his shoulders asking him to come for a beer. Only bloody thighs, hard stares and sneers of disdain. This was unfamiliar territory for Dirk, whose resolve to leave Gattan crystallised with each passing week.

Once he was home, Dirk took two Panadol and texted Hayley to see if she was keen to swing by KFC. He picked her up in the Monaro half an hour later. She was still moving gingerly, but most of her wounds had healed. The drive-thru was busy. Dirk navigated the Monaro through a queue of Commodores and Subarus driven by young men he vaguely recognised, who had graduated a year or two ahead of him. He ordered a Zinger Stacker meal. Hayley opted for a Maxi Popcorn Chicken Combo.

'You know that's not actual chicken,' Dirk told her.

'I'd rather this than a greasy leg,' Hayley said. 'I've been struggling lately with meat that's still in the shape of a murdered sentient creature.'

'Chickens don't have brains,' Dirk said, driving out of the car park and heading for the coast road.

'You really didn't pay attention in class, eh?'

'You know what I mean,' Dirk said. 'They don't have minds. They can't think.'

'You mean they're not self-aware?' Hayley asked.

'Right. A chicken doesn't know it's a chicken.'

'I think, therefore I peck,' Hayley said, biting into one of the popcorn balls. 'To be honest, Dirk, I'm not a hundred per cent certain *you're* self-aware.'

'Everyone's been acting like I don't matter around here, so maybe you're right,' Dirk said.

'Aw, struggling to make new boyfriends?'

'It's been a challenging couple of months,' Dirk admitted.

'Tell me about it. You haven't heard from Jess, I take it?'

'Radio silence,' Dirk said. 'You?'

'Same,' Hayley told him. 'I can understand her blanking you, but I thought she'd get over my thing.'

Dirk shook his head, indicated and took the turn off to Outlook Beach.

'It's not like it wasn't obvious,' he said.

Hayley reeled in the passenger seat.

'Fuck off,' she said. 'You had no idea I was into girls.'

'Yeah, I did,' Dirk said, pulling into a parking space and cutting the engine. He wound down the window and breathed in the sea air.

'Please explain,' Hayley said.

'You knocked me back that time I tried to pash you at Amy Webb's seventeenth.'

'Jesus, Dirk,' Hayley said, shaking her head. 'Just because a woman refuses your advances doesn't mean she's gay.'

'Well, you're the only one who ever has, so . . .'

'Right, well, fair point but in future, don't assume that,' Hayley told him. 'God, your ego.'

'Took a bruising today,' Dirk said, showing her the contusion on the back of his hand.

'Gattan get smashed?' Hayley asked.

'Yeah, and so did I. Those blokes aren't exactly welcoming.'

'You never did have many friends,' Hayley said casually. Dirk frowned as he bit into his burger, holding it over the box to ensure sauce didn't drip onto his jeans. He thought back over his teenage years and realised that Hayley was right. Other than with Jess and Hayley, his friendships had been temporary and infrequent.

'Too focused on girls, maybe,' he admitted. 'That a bad thing?'

Hayley shrugged. 'Not necessarily. Maybe you were preparing for life after school. Everything changes, eh? You realise that you're kind of on your own.'

'You have someone now,' Dirk said. 'How is she, anyway?'

'Early days,' Hayley said. 'Still getting my head around it.'

'We going to see her down here in Gattan?'

'A lesbian Asian in Gattan,' Hayley said, trying the thought on for size. 'I don't think this town is ready for that. Maybe in a decade. Maybe never.'

'Yeah, fuck this place,' Dirk said.

'You and Jess were going to travel, weren't you?' Hayley said. 'Guess that's knocked on the head. You planning an overseas trip with Lucy?'

Dirk shook his head. 'Nah, not her bag. Was thinking of going by myself once I've saved a bit of cash. Do the backpacker thing, maybe work in a pub in London, fool around with exotic women from twenty-six different countries. I could visit the Netherlands, link up with the cousins I've never seen. Come with me. They have dykes there.'

Hayley groaned. 'That's a terrible excuse for a joke,' she said.

Dirk laughed. 'At least I can make it now,' he said, whacking her playfully on the arm.

'Try harder next time,' she said then sighed. 'As appealing as a gap year sounds, I have no money. I'm applying for jobs in the city. Café work, mostly, but I'll take whatever I can get.'

'Move into a share house and live the dream,' Dirk said. 'Keep a room free for me. I might join you when I get back.'

'You not taking over the business, then?'

'Jack of the fucking place already,' Dirk said. 'I'm cheap labour and he's a mean old bastard. I'm not going to spend the best years of my life stuck behind a counter replacing watch batteries.'

'Lucy might object to you taking off for a year of hedonism,' Hayley suggested.

Having finished his burger, Dirk started in on the hot chips.

'She's a temporary distraction,' he said. Hayley glared at him disapprovingly. 'I know, I know. I shouldn't have broken up with Jess, but she was getting too attached.'

'God forbid she follow her heart.'

'If you want to get soppy,' Dirk said. 'Can I help it if my heart is so huge that it's capable of loving a thousand women?'

'There's that ego again. That's exactly the sort of thing unfaithful men say.' Hayley adopted a faux bashful voice. 'It's not my fault I'm so adorable and women fall at my feet.'

'Well, it isn't,' Dirk said.

Hayley threw up her hands in frustration, then opened the passenger door and stepped out into the warm embrace of the evening.

'I'm going for a walk,' she said.

'Wait, I'll come with you,' Dirk said, grabbing the remainder of his chips.

'Give me all your rubbish,' Hayley told him.

Dirk cleaned out the car. In addition to the KFC wrappers, he discovered an empty takeaway coffee cup and a chocolate Big M rolling around on the floor behind the driver's seat. He handed it all to Hayley. She gathered the garbage in her arms and squeezed it into the already full public bin.

∗ ∗ ∗

THE CLOSEST CINEMA TO GATTAN WAS THE MULTIPLEX IN Langdale, an outer suburb ninety minutes away. Mobile speed cameras lurked along the length of the highway, ready to catch country motorists who dared to venture even a whisker above the speed limit. Dirk was pinged several times that summer, drawing hefty fines and nine demerit points. Each time it happened, he railed against a system he believed raised revenue to be frittered away on vanity infrastructure projects while the roads remained full of potholes that had almost claimed his life on several occasions. Given the perils associated with an otherwise humdrum trip to the movies, Dirk only caved when Lucy insisted.

It was almost midnight when Dirk finally got home after one such outing. They had seen *Meet the Fockers*. Dirk would have preferred *Blade: Trinity*, but that was never going to happen. He dropped Lucy at the end of her parents' driveway in Venus Creek and groaned when he checked the time. His father was still awake when Dirk entered the lounge room, watching a western he had recorded earlier in the week. Dirk's mother had long since retired to bed.

'You've got work in the morning,' Willem said when Dirk dropped his car keys in a dish by the door.

Dirk shrugged, unwilling to dignify the statement with a response.

'Clint Eastwood?' he asked, perching on the arm of the sofa.

'*High Plains Drifter*,' Willem replied. 'His character is a demon.'

'Cool,' Dirk said. He didn't share his father's obsession with westerns and science fiction movies.

'I need you to work over lunch tomorrow to cover breaks,' Willem said. 'And I want you to stay after five, so you can watch me service that Bulova.'

'It's hardly a spectator sport, Dad,' Dirk said.

'You need to learn.'

Dirk was at the end of his rope. 'If I'm doing overtime, I want extra pay,' he said. 'In fact, I need a pay rise. I could earn more stacking shelves at Coles.'

Willem regarded his son with cool detachment, then reached for the remote and paused the movie. The screen froze on Eastwood riding into a dusty town on a pale horse.

'Why do you need money?' he asked.

'I'm saving to go overseas,' Dirk said. 'I've told you that a hundred times already.'

'You're lucky I pay you at all,' Willem says. 'Your salary comes out of profits, which are lean at the moment. Our family has worked with timepieces for generations. You should be grateful that I'm teaching you the trade. It's a highly skilled profession.'

Dirk went to reply, but Willem held up a finger to indicate he wasn't finished.

'Forget these ideas of travelling overseas,' he said. 'You're not going anywhere. I'll slice your passport in two and sell that shitbox car of yours to the wreckers. You need to knuckle down and focus on the business so that when you take over, I can rest easy knowing a century of graft hasn't been for nothing.'

'Are you done?' Dirk asked. 'Can I speak now?'

'By all means,' Willem said.

'If I ever take over the business – and that's a big "if", Dad – I'm going to pay myself a generous salary. I'm not slogging my guts out just to squirrel a few bucks away for a rainy day that will never come. The profits will be mine to enjoy as I see fit. Removing links from watch straps is a piece of piss. A monkey could do it. You should be concentrating on high-profit items like gemstones, but you're so stuck in your ways you've forgotten how to run a successful business, if you ever even knew. That business was handed to you on a silver platter by Grandad.' Dirk raised himself to his full height. 'And by the way, I'll go wherever the fuck I want, and you won't stop me.'

'Is that so?' Willem said, carefully placing the remote on the coffee table and standing up. Willem van der Saar was an imposing figure. Dirk was broad-shouldered and athletic, but Willem was twenty kilograms heavier. The man cracked his knuckles and stretched out the cricks in his neck.

Dirk knew what was coming. It had happened countless times before. Of late, Dirk had been holding his own. He'd come to accept the grim truth: the physical abuse would only stop when his father was defeated.

Willem's bulk belied his speed. He feinted a left hook and Dirk stepped to the right, but his path was blocked by the standard lamp. Blinded by the glare of the bulb, Dirk didn't see the slap coming. Willem's callused hand landed square on Dirk's cheek, causing the young man to stumble against the wall and slide to the floor in shock. It was the hardest his father had ever hit him, and it stung like a bull ant bite.

One punch was usually enough to impart the lesson, but not this time. Dirk had injured his father's pride and besmirched the family name. As he rolled onto all fours, moving to get up, Willem kicked his son in the ribs. The fact that he was wearing Target slippers softened the blow, but it still came as a shock. His father had never kicked him while he was down before. He flashed back to the casual cruelty he had encountered on the footy field and a red mist descended.

When Willem tried to kick his son again, Dirk morphed into ruckman mode, grabbed his father's leg and rolled up his body. His old footy coach had taught him that was the best way to put someone down when they were sinking the boot into you. Dirk lashed out with an elbow as his dad fell to the carpet, catching him in the throat as he pivoted to straddle the larger man. In a frenzy, he punched his father twice in the face, hardly able to believe he was doing so. Willem absorbed the blows as if they were nothing and jabbed a knee upwards towards Dirk's balls, bucking him off. The man's strength shocked Dirk, who scooted away across the rug, upending the coffee table in the process.

Willem van der Saar sat up and leant back against the sofa. He was breathing heavily, struggling for air, a trickle of blood at the corner of his lips. He glared at his son.

'Unbelievable lack of respect,' he said. 'I thought we raised you better than that.'

'Shut up!' Dirk said, rubbing his aching jaw with trembling fingers. 'I'm eighteen, Dad. You're not the boss of me anymore. I'm not like you.'

'That much is obvious,' Willem said. 'No work ethic, no direction, and you fight like a coward.'

'Just so we're clear,' Dirk said as he hauled himself to his feet, 'this will happen every time you lay a hand on me from now on. Eventually, you'll wind up in emergency. I can promise you that.'

Willem snarled and moved to get up for another round when Dirk's mother entered the room.

'What's all the banging and crashing down here?' she said, eyeballing Dirk. 'Do you know what time it is?'

'Time for me to leave,' Dirk said. The remote control had fallen at Dirk's feet. He kicked it, sending the remote skittering under the couch.

'I expect you in the shop by eight, boy,' Willem shouted, as Dirk scooped up his keys and slammed the door behind him.

The Monaro's engine was still warm. It started on the first go. Dirk left a trail of burnt rubber on the driveway as he screeched out into Jongebloed Lane. It was a fifteen-minute drive to Windmill Creek. Once he was out of town, Dirk slowed down. Thrashing the car would do it no good, and at that late hour there was often wildlife on the coast road. Just before the dirt road turnoff, the silhouette of an echidna appeared in the headlight beams. Dirk stopped to let the animal cross, watching it waddle into the bush on the other side.

The dashboard clock read twelve-forty when he pulled into the car park overlooking the creek. Dirk switched off the ignition and sat there for a while, listening to the engine pinging as it cooled. He rummaged in the glove compartment until he found an old pack of smokes Jess had left there six months earlier. There were two cigarettes in the crumpled packet. He extracted one and lit it, getting out of the car and leaning against the door as he inhaled. He coughed twice and then stubbed it out. He'd never enjoyed smoking, had only ever done so to please his ex. He wandered away from the car, along a faint trail until it turned sandy underfoot. There was a grassy knoll overlooking the creek. Dirk sat there, watching the water flowing between the dunes to the sea.

He catalogued his injuries, sustained on the football field and at home. He ached all over, but he was used to the pain. He had endured it for so many years, he had assimilated the discomfort, learnt to live with it. He thought about Willem van der Saar and Lodewijk van der Saar and all the other Van der Saar men who had come to that godforsaken corner of the world and claimed it as their own. Dirk wasn't like them. He didn't want to become like them. Gattan was his prison. He had served eighteen years' hard labour, no time off for good behaviour, no chance of parole. All he needed was a few thousand dollars for airfare and some initial spending money. He had an EU passport. Didn't even need a visa. He could live wherever he wanted. Tour the Greek islands. Rave in Ibiza. Sunbake on a nude beach in Croatia. Bide his time. Work in Europe until his father died, then return and claim the inheritance. Sell the business, sell the house, set his mother up in one of the old miner's cottages and then take off. Rent an apartment in New York. Catch a train through Mexico. Become a nomad. Spend half a year in a beach shack in Guatemala. Buy a motorbike and ride to the tip of the continent, see the Strait of Magellan just like he and Jess had planned. Except he'd be alone, free and unencumbered.

Dirk took a breath of sea air. He was nearly there. So close he could almost touch it. Another six months of saving and he'd have enough money to leave town. As he looked out across the dark Southern Ocean, it amused him to think that one day, half a year from then, the residents of Gattan would awaken to yet another monotonous morning, the same as the one before in every respect except one. Dirk van der Saar would be gone – he'd have fled to a faraway place where no one knew his name.

* * *

THE MONARO IDLED AS DIRK WAITED BY THE END OF THE driveway for Lucy. The entrance to the Moore property was on an awkward corner. Dirk had driven over the cattle grid and then performed a tricky three-point turn so the car was facing the road. Although Lucy's parents knew their daughter was going out with him, Dirk preferred to minimise contact with them. He didn't like the way Angie Moore regarded him, as if she were sizing up his prospective wealth. Bert Moore resorted to the timeworn protective father's trick of attempting to crush Dirk's fingers whenever they shook hands. They acted like the King and Queen of Venus Creek, which they were, in a way. To avoid feeling like a medieval suitor every time he picked Lucy up, Dirk texted her when he arrived, and waited for his date to walk the length of the dirt road. On other occasions, they would meet at the pub, which was a twenty-minute walk from the farmhouse across the back paddocks.

Lucy jumped into the passenger seat and flung her arms around Dirk's neck, showering him with kisses.

'Steady on,' Dirk said. 'At least let me get us to the beach before you ravish me.'

'Hello to you, too,' Lucy said, clicking her seatbelt on.

Dirk edged the Monaro out onto the road and headed south, towards the coast and Outlook Beach. Spiderbait's 'Take Me Back' blasted from the sound system. They made small talk as they drove. Lucy positively glowed with delight at being out in the world with her beau.

'You think we should move in together?' she asked, out of the blue.

'It's a bit soon,' Dirk said hesitantly. He was stunned by the suggestion; they hadn't discussed co-habitation before. 'Besides, I don't have enough money for my own place.'

'I could live with you and your parents,' Lucy suggested.

'Yeah, you don't want that,' Dirk told her.

'Oh, I don't know,' Lucy said. 'If it means we get to spend every night together, I'm game to give it a try.'

Dirk thought back to what his mother had said a few hours earlier. She had sidled up to him after dinner, while he was washing the dishes.

'Your father and I approve,' she said, enigmatically.

'Of what?' Dirk said, surprised they'd endorse anything he did.

'Lucy Moore,' Carole said.

'It's a casual thing,' Dirk said. 'You know me, Mum. Just another notch on the belt.'

'You Van der Saar men,' Carole said, squeezing his arm. As she scoured the cupboard for the Rooibos tea her husband liked, Dirk felt disquieted by the notion that in bedding the young women of Gattan he might be following in his father's sordid footsteps. It was difficult to imagine the old man courting. He rarely showed Dirk's mother the slightest affection.

'It's surprising the Moore and Van der Saar clans haven't forged a blood alliance long before now,' Carole said as she put the kettle on.

'I'm not Henry the Eighth, Mum,' Dirk said.

Carole laughed. 'No,' she said. 'But Lucy Moore holds a lot more appeal than some of the tramps you drive out to that beach, like that repugnant Jessica Barry.'

'Jess was all right,' Dirk replied. 'And how do you know about . . .'

'Gattan is a small town, Dirk,' his mother said. 'I know everyone's business.'

Dirk told Lucy they should table the idea of moving in together for the time being and simply enjoy each other's company. Lucy sulked a little, but her mood changed when they pulled into the car park overlooking the beach. There was one other vehicle there, but it reversed and drove away just as Dirk parked. It was already nine o'clock. A brisk wind swept along the beach, causing whirling sand eddies.

Lucy and Dirk made out for a while.

'Back seat?' Dirk suggested breathlessly.

Lucy gripped Dirk's stubbled jawline in her hands, her eyes rolled back. She snapped out of her rapture and let him go, clawing at the doorhandle.

'I have a better idea,' she said. 'Let's go for a dip.'

'It's a bit chilly out there, Luce,' Dirk said. 'Summer's over.'

'I'll make it worth your while,' Lucy said, arching her eyebrows suggestively.

By the time Dirk dragged himself out of the warmth of the car, Lucy was already charging down the dune towards the sea. Once she reached the flat sand at the bottom, she paused to awkwardly strip off her clothes. Dirk snorted as he watched her hopping around, tugging at her uncooperative jeans. Eventually she sat on the sand and kicked her clothes into a pile. She leapt to her feet and raised her arms to the sky, spinning around.

'Get down here!' she shouted.

Dirk walked down the dune, gaining pace and almost falling towards the bottom. Lucy ran over and wrapped herself around him. Her skin was cold and covered in goosebumps.

'You're mad,' he told her, laughing.

Lucy disengaged and took off, charging across the sand to the water. As she plunged headlong into the surf, Dirk's mind photographed the image: a slender, naked woman disappearing into the roiling waves under the pale light of a crescent moon. Lucy surfaced and stood up, water to her waist. She shook her hair and squealed at the cold.

Like a mermaid, Dirk thought absent-mindedly as he undressed. Once he was naked, he waded tentatively into the sea. Lucy extended her arms towards him.

'Jesus, it's freezing,' he said as they embraced.

Lucy kissed him passionately. Dirk ran his tongue around her neck, licking the salt. Lucy moaned and gripped his hair. It was impossible to fuck in the surf, so they pressed tightly against each other instead, bathing in each other's warmth as they were pummelled by waves. Lucy ran so hot Dirk was surprised the water didn't evaporate in a cloud of steam when it touched her skin. He buried his face in her wet hair and whispered something he had promised himself he would never say to a woman.

'What was that?' Lucy said. 'What did you just say?'

'Nothing,' Dirk told her. 'You know.'

They stared at each other for a full five seconds, an eternity, and then they kissed, slowly this time, with intent. Dirk felt the beat of her heart as her chest pressed against his.

'I'm pregnant,' Lucy said.

Dirk reeled back, his head abruptly filled with static.

'What?' he said.

'I'm pregnant,' Lucy repeated, a wrinkle forming in the faultless skin of her forehead.

'I don't understand how,' Dirk said. Her fingers suddenly felt icy cold on his neck.

'We fuck constantly. What did you think would happen?'

The scolding expression on Lucy's face terrified Dirk.

'I know, but aren't you on the pill?' Dirk stammered. He knew it sounded weak as soon as he heard the words tumbling out of his mouth. He had trusted her to take responsibility for contraception. Big mistake.

'I stopped taking it ages ago,' Lucy explained. 'Mum said it was bad for my reproductive health.'

Dirk nodded dumbly.

'I thought you'd be more pleased, to be honest,' Lucy said.

A huge wave chose that moment to hit them side-on. They staggered and let go of each other, but neither fell. When they faced each other again, Lucy had her arms wrapped around her chest and was shivering.

'Of course I'm pleased,' Dirk said, the phrase falling from his lips with barely any conviction. 'I just need a minute, Luce. It's a lot to take in. I wasn't expecting this.'

'I want to call her Sky, if it's a girl,' Lucy said.

Dirk forced a smile. He may have been a bastard, but he wasn't a monster. He waded through the surf and pulled her close. Lucy threw her arms around his neck and kissed him, relieved and happy. Dirk looked over her shoulder at the horizon, glowing purple where air and water met.

For a fleeting moment, Dirk considered running, but he knew it wouldn't matter, that he'd have to come back eventually. There was no way out. Dirk van der Saar, undone by hubris, Hayley would say when she found out. It was bound to happen sooner or later. And Jess, well, she would be incandescent and frustrated that she hadn't thought of it first.

Dirk began to sob. Lucy whispered softly in Dirk's ear as he wept, telling him that everything would be fine because they were together, they had each other and that she would always be there for him, just as he would be for her. That this was right, this was meant to be, this was their destiny.

Dirk raised his eyes to the stars. So many worlds he would never know. He'd been so close.

* * *

DIRK DECIDED TO TELL HIS PARENTS THE NEXT DAY, OVER SUNDAY lunch. He didn't sleep well, and turmoil continued to churn within him all morning. It was as if he were sleepwalking, the volume of the world lowered to a persistent hum. He considered saying nothing, but if it was real, if he and Lucy were to have a child together, then plans had to be made, wheels set in motion. A wedding. A place to live. Dreams had to be kicked to the kerb.

'You've hardly touched the chicken,' Carole said. 'What's wrong with you? Are you sick?'

Dirk woozily regarded his parents across the dining room table. He felt drunk. Wished he was.

'He knows,' Willem said, looking smug. 'She must have told him last night.'

Dirk snapped out of his trance and gawped at his father in disbelief. Carole leant across and patted his arm.

'We're so pleased for you both,' she said.

Dirk forced himself to swallow the mashed potato he'd been swirling around in his mouth. He glanced between his parents' grinning faces.

'You knew?' he said. 'Before me?'

'I told you, I know everything that goes on in this town,' Carole said. 'Angie Moore called me when she found out. We've been on tenterhooks waiting for that poor girl to muster the courage to tell you.'

'This has nothing to do with you,' Dirk protested, dropping his cutlery on the plate. 'It's my business.'

'On the contrary,' Willem said. 'Bert and I have had several lengthy discussions about how best to proceed. They were hesitant about you at first, but I presented a compelling case. I went in to bat for you, boy. You should be thanking me.'

A supernova exploded inside Dirk's head. His vision clouded, the figures seated at the table blurred into hazy shapes.

'But . . . it's not fair.'

'As far as we're concerned this is the best possible outcome,' Carole said. 'Angie and Bert agree. They don't have a son, and they couldn't ask for a better candidate, Dirk. No one wants an outsider coming into Gattan and claiming all that land. This way, ownership remains local.'

'Ownership,' Dirk said, reduced to parroting his mother's words.

'Good for the Van der Saar business, too,' Willem said. 'No more shirking of responsibilities, swanning around the world like some scallywag. Once you've done right by that girl, I'll increase your salary and we'll find you a place to live. You can shadow me until I retire, and then it's all yours, son. This was always the plan.'

'Your father and I want to buy a caravan and travel around Australia,' Carole said. 'See the country while we're still young.'

Dirk nodded, his lips upturned in a rictus. He had nothing more to say. A galaxy swirled behind his eyes, an inky curtain of infinite blackness punctuated with a million iridescent points of aimless light. He had never felt so small, so insignificant, so powerless.

'Come to the shop early tomorrow, son,' Willem said, smiling. 'You've got a lot to learn.'

PART SEVEN

KINGDOM OF HADES

THE BATTERED LANDCRUISER PULLED OFF THE HIGHWAY TO Langdale at Jumbuk service station, or what was left of it. Mostly just a black scorch mark on the concrete. After the bowsers exploded in a plume of flame that could be seen fifty kilometres away at the time, the subsequent fire had razed the truck stop. Such was the intensity of the inferno, the nearby bitumen had melted and re-formed as a series of warped ridges in the road, rendering that side of the highway virtually impassable. Five people lost their lives that day, including two teenagers working in the adjoining McCafé.

The LandCruiser mounted the kerb and crossed the patch of scorched grass, bumping back down onto the forecourt and circling the rusted wreckage of four vehicles before slowing to a halt next to a row of sedge grass that had flourished since the fire. Enough time had passed since the explosion that fresh tendrils were sprouting, a spattering of green poking through jagged cracks in the concrete.

Jess cut the engine and stepped out of the vehicle to stretch. Baz Luhrmann jumped down, shook himself from jowls to tail and took off at a sprint across the car park. He halted by a blackened stump to raise his leg and mark territory.

Jess was wearing black combat boots, dark blue utility pants festooned with zipped pockets, a plain white T-shirt and a blue Hurley-branded baseball cap. She removed the hat and ran her hand across the buzzcut beneath, scratching her sweaty scalp with short nails, then she raised her face to bask in the November sunlight. Summer was on the way, although spring rains persisted. She checked the time on her watch and leant back into the cabin to grab her water bottle. She was early. The others would be there soon. In the meantime, she would wait and enjoy the silence of the bombsite.

Two hundred and fifty-four days had passed since the initial event. Nothing had changed, and everything was broken. Jess had long since stopped paying attention to the news cycle, but when last she checked, thirty-six nations had been embroiled in civil unrest. There had been violent uprisings, bloody revolutions, brutal responses from beleaguered authority figures. Several governments had been deposed, and the replacement regimes fared no better. India and Pakistan were at war. Millions were starving across Europe and Asia. America had run out of fuel. The song of Orpheus continued to be heard every day, as hundreds of thousands of children reached their ninth birthdays and aged no further. Societies everywhere had split into factions. Primary schools were abandoned as parents kept their children at home. The remote places of the world were swamped by desperate parents trying to isolate their kids from the strange, melancholy, relentless plague for which no solution had been found. No cure, no vaccine, no hope.

Under intense pressure, the Australian prime minister had stepped down. His replacement, a party man with a bellyful of empty promises, only lasted eighteen days. He was trampled to death by a crowd of angry parents outside Parliament House. A fragile order was restored across the nation by a reluctant military, many of whom had themselves suffered unimaginable losses. For the most part, Australia had become a lawless place. Its cities were in chaos. Thousands of products were no longer available. Only country towns enjoyed some semblance of normality, despite the weird, permanent gaps on supermarket shelves. Many had become independent vassals, producing their own food and rejecting outsiders and the need for luxuries. The mains power grid was in a constant state of flux. Those with home solar congratulated themselves for unwittingly preparing for the crisis. This ongoing atmosphere of disaster was a breeding ground for conspiracy, opportunity and reprisal.

The next car to arrive was Georgia Slater's clapped-out green Ford Falcon. She was running a spare wheel on the rear right side. She pulled in next to the LandCruiser and stepped out, blinking at the cerulean sky, then turned back and fished through the centre console for a pair of sunglasses. Schnitzel the dachshund scrabbled out of the car, barking as she ran to meet her friend Baz. They sniffed each other, tails wagging, before peeling away at high speed towards the nearest overgrown paddock. Georgia lit a cigarette and joined Jess, who by this stage was squatting on the kerb.

'Hey, mate,' Jess said. 'You shouldn't be smoking at a petrol station, you know.'

Georgia laughed, sucking deeply on the cigarette and blowing a huge plume of smoke in the air.

'Must have been a sight when it went up, eh? Shame we didn't think of it first.'

'The media blamed it on us anyway.' Jess shrugged, and nodded towards Georgia's spare wheel. 'Those are designed to be temporary.'

'I know,' Georgia said. 'New tyres are hard to come by now. How many are we expecting today?'

'Ten,' Jess said. 'City girls, mostly, from a new chapter.'

'We should start charging for this service.'

'What are they going to pay us with, toilet paper?'

'You see today's figures?' Georgia asked.

'I don't look at them,' Jess said.

'Not the O9 stats, the number of loo-roll related fatalities. There's an app that keeps track. It's called Rolled.'

Jess smirked. 'Sick, but funny,' she said. 'How many people were rolled today?'

'Twelve, reported. You have to take your laughs where you can get them,' Georgia said, as a Transit van approached from the direction of Langdale.

'Better direct them in, so they don't hit the potholes and snap an axle they can't replace,' Jess suggested.

Georgia dropped her cigarette and stubbed it out. She jogged to the edge of the highway and waved her arms, signalling the van to slow down and pull into the truck stop.

The vehicle parked next to Georgia's Falcon and disgorged the new arrivals. They stretched legs, arms and backs. Several convened discreetly in the long grass to urinate. The driver approached Jess, who rose to meet her.

'Nicky Pritchard,' she said, extending her right arm to show Jess the trident tattoo on the inside of her wrist. Jess rolled her forearm. Her skin was marked with the same symbol.

'Jess Ward,' she introduced herself. 'Thanks for coming. Any trouble?'

'Nope,' Nicky said. 'Clear run out of the city. Roads are deserted.'

'No drones on the scanner?'

'There's another outage this morning,' Nicky told her. 'Everything's down. No one knows we're here.'

'All right, good,' Jess said. 'Gather the sistren, please, mate.'

Nicky rounded up the new arrivals, who formed a line before Jess. Georgia performed a quick check to make sure everyone had the trident tattoo, rubbing the skin on their wrists to check for fakes. ASIO had attempted to infiltrate Kingdom of Hades on numerous occasions, with varying success. An entire chapter of thirty Orpheans in South Australia had been unceremoniously carted off to an Orpheanage in black vans after their meeting was raided.

Jess crossed her arms and surveyed the recruits. The women were a variety of ages and ethnicities, but all shared a haunted look of grim determination.

'I'm Jess Ward, regional south-eastern chapter,' she began. 'I'll be your field operations training facilitator. As you may know, we're planning a significant local action. Some of you may be able to participate in that, although leadership informs me that most of you will be assigned elsewhere after you've completed these exercises. Now, before we go any further, let's take a moment to mourn our Niners.' She held a palm over her heart. 'Tyler.'

Georgia went next, placing her hand on her chest too. 'Pippa,' she said.

The recruits each named their Niner in this manner: Isaac. Wei. Charlotte. Vihaan. Aisha. Harrison. Yasmin. Evie. Gitanjali. Zhiyu.

A moment's silence was observed for the fallen.

Jess was about to speak again when one of the mothers raised a hand.

'Yes?' Jess asked.

'Do we get uniforms?'

A few of the others looked embarrassed at the question. Jess tried her best to sound informative without being patronising.

'Kingdom of Hades is an internationally recognised terror organisation,' she said. 'Our sistren overseas have toppled governments, destroyed critical infrastructure and been responsible for the assassination of corrupt Decadian politicians and community leaders. We operate in the shadows, and if any of us are detained, we vow silence. We're classified as dangerous extremists. So, no, there are no cute uniforms.'

'Sorry,' the woman said, blushing. 'I just thought maybe for the training camp?'

Jess inhaled wearily and glanced at Georgia, who answered for her.

'We can provide coveralls, if you're worried about getting your designer jeans dirty.'

This caustic comment resulted in a few sniggers.

'Hard Yakka shut up shop,' Georgia added. 'We have to make do with what we can get.'

'All right, let me ask you lot some questions,' Jess said. She picked out a recruit at random, an Indian woman wearing an oversized black bomber jacket. 'Tell me about the cycle of nine.'

The woman raised her head with pride.

'The number nine represents completion,' she said. 'Not an ending, but the fulfilment of a cycle, an acknowledgment of life's ebb and flow. A chance to begin anew.'

'Excellent,' Jess said, then pointed to a young woman in dungarees and pink Converse sneakers. 'What does it mean to walk the path of nine?'

The woman gulped, then cleared her throat.

'Those on the path of nine are generous, passionate and creative. They stand for the rights of others. They serve the community. Their purpose is aligned with a greater universal need and truth.'

'What else?' Jess said. Hands were raised. She picked responders at random.

'They seek to interpret the chaos of this world.'

'They are passionate and ambitious, qualities that, when properly channelled, enable them to become powerful champions of justice.'

'They have unfinished business.'

Jess held up her hands for quiet.

'Absolutely fucking right,' she said. 'Our numbers swell with each passing day as more innocent lives are claimed. We know who is responsible for this curse. Who is it? Tell me, who's behind the scourge?'

Many voices spoke at once.

'The Decadians!'

'The elites!'

'The parents of the final generation!'

Jess nodded.

'Yes, sisters, it is those who have the most to gain. We shall not stand idly by. We have been drawn into the cycle of nine for a reason. We are agents of renewal and our cause is just. We must learn to harness our grief. We must take up arms and redress the wrongs perpetrated upon us by those malign forces intoxicated by their own power. We will shape the future in our image, not theirs.' Jess paused to let her words sink in. 'If we stand united, nothing can stop us.'

Several of the recruits were swaying, giddy with the weight of belonging, infused with a sense of righteousness.

'Eyes front!' Jess shouted. 'Towards a new world.'

'Don't look back, don't look back, don't look back,' the recruits chanted.

After the applause had subsided, Jess told the women to fall out and take ten before they proceeded to the training camp. The group dispersed, exchanging supportive hugs and breaking out cigarettes and snacks. Nicky approached Jess and whistled in admiration.

'Some speech,' she said. 'No wonder leadership sent us to you.'

'It's from the handbook,' Jess said dismissively.

'Still powerful,' Georgia said.

'Helps if you believe what you're saying,' Jess explained. 'Hey, Nicky, I need you to make a list for me.'

Nicky nodded enthusiastically and pulled out her phone.

'No,' Jess said curtly. 'Write it down, pen and paper. You can't eat your phone if you get caught.'

'It has facial recognition security and a passcode,' she said.

'Then they'll mash it against your face and torture the code out of you,' Jess said.

'Hold on,' Nicky said, then went back to the van. She returned a moment later with a notepad and pen. Jess dictated a list of ingredients.

'I want each of the recruits to obtain a single item off that list in the coming week,' she said. 'That way, no one person will draw too much attention to themselves.'

'That's a shit ton of ammonium nitrate,' Nicky said. 'Where will we source that?'

'Buying that much fertiliser from Bunnings will raise a red flag,' Georgia agreed.

'Bunnings is still operating out here?' Nicky asked, surprised.

'Ours is,' Georgia nodded. 'Independent local business now.'

'I know a farm where we can get what we need,' Jess said. 'Don't worry about it.'

'Wood pulp, saltpetre and ethylene glycol dinitrate,' Nicky said, eyes widening as the penny dropped. 'Holy shit. Where'd you get this formula?'

'Kingdom of Hades dark website,' Jess told her. 'They also have a killer saltless raspberry and white chocolate muffin recipe. Helps transition newbies.'

'They all become us, eventually,' Georgia said.

Shrieks of alarm issued from the recruits as Baz Luhrmann bounded out of the long grass by the highway and pelted across the melted bitumen. Abandoned domestic animals turned feral were a problem all over the country. With so many families broken, pets had been left to fend for themselves.

'It's all right, he's with us,' Georgia reassured the women.

In his excitement at meeting so many new people, Baz Luhrmann's rear end shook with such ferocity that he fell over three times while everyone patted him. Georgia peered across the road, looking for her dachshund. Schnitzel emerged from the grass a moment later, carrying what appeared to be a long stick in her mouth. The dog struggled to keep her chin up with the weight of the trophy. Georgia shook her head in dismay.

'Always bringing home sticks ten times bigger than her,' she said.

'That's not a stick, mate,' Jess said.

As the dachshund padded across the scorched forecourt, it became clear she was carrying a snake in her mouth. The reptile's head and tail dragged along the concrete either side of the dog. Baz Luhrmann ran to Schnitzel and grabbed one end of the dead snake, trying to wrestle it from the jaws of his friend. A tug of war ensued, and the dogs wound up with half a snake each.

'Drop it, drop it,' Georgia shouted. Schnitzel was reluctant to give up her prize, but at Jess's command, Baz Luhrmann brought his end of the snake over and placed it obediently at her feet. Jess crouched to examine the serpent, while the new recruits gathered round.

'What kind is that?' one of the city girls asked, horrified.

'Red-bellied black,' Jess told them. 'Sun brings them out.'

'Are they venomous?'

'Extremely, but not aggressive,' Jess explained. 'You probably won't get bitten, unless you're unlucky.'

'Or a dog,' Georgia said, brandishing the other half of the snake. Blood dripped from its midsection where Baz Luhrmann's canines had severed the creature in two. Georgia pulled her arm back to throw the remains into the paddock.

'Don't,' Jess said, grabbing her by the wrist. 'The dogs will just run after it, and besides, that's good eating.'

One of the city recruits wrinkled her nose in disgust. Jess gathered up both halves of the snake and wrapped them in a plastic bag.

'Hard times, ladies,' she explained to the appalled recruits. 'If you're trying to evade capture, this is what you might have to eat. You'll be learning this sort of thing on the course. Best get your head around it now.'

'You said they were poisonous,' one of the recruits protested.

'Venomous. There's a difference. Venom gland is in the head. Sever that and you can eat the rest. It's lean meat, low in fat. Cook it over an open fire and you've got yourself a hearty saltless meal.'

'What does it taste like?'

Jess gave the recruit a wry smile.

'Chicken.'

* * *

THE RED-BRICK POST OFFICE BUILDING COMPRISED LITTLE MORE than a counter, a disconnected rotary telephone, several noticeboards and a tiny office where the postmaster would have sat, sorting mail for the miners who lived in the smattering of bluestone cottages on site. These humble abodes had withstood the vagaries of time and, although they were cold, they provided good shelter, and Jess permitted fires after nightfall. Once the mine had closed, it was converted into a museum, but it was never popular. Gattan was too far off the beaten track, and modern tourists were not interested in such a grim reminder of yesteryear. The museum folded in the 1980s and had lain derelict ever since.

With their vehicles hidden inside the spacious stable that once housed half-a-dozen pit ponies, the Kingdom of Hades cell was undetectable. The names of the horses were listed on a faded chart pinned to the stable wall. They were called things like Pacer, Mitch, Cobber and Doodle, along with several racist monikers unsettling to contemporary ears.

Jess taught the women basic survival skills, along with stealth tactics and how to follow someone in a two-person team without being spotted. The recruits slept on camp beds in the old cottages. They cooked and ate together. They washed their clothing and bathed in a nearby creek. Many of the kitchen items were put to use, still valuable more than a century later. It only took a few days for the city dwellers to adapt. While some grumbled at the hardship, everyone eventually embraced their new-found sense of self-reliance and independence. This was a better way to live. Uncluttered. Delineated. Jess was confident the recruits would emerge from the training camp with a startling clarity of purpose.

On the fourth day, she split them into two rival teams. Five were tasked with defending the post office from incursion, supervised by Georgia. They were assigned timed patrols to simulate security patterns typical of any large infrastructure or governmental site. The remaining five were the infiltration squad, guided by Jess. Their objective was to break into the post office and recover a tin of Colombian coffee beans from a locked cupboard. If they were successful, the infiltrators could grind and brew coffee the next morning. This was an attractive prize. Imported beans had largely disappeared from Australian supermarket shelves. If the team were caught, however, they had to spend the night in a makeshift underground prison just inside the mouth of the mine. No sleeping bags or candles. Georgia's squad were granted no incentives. They were simply to act as efficient guards.

Having briefed her team on how best to proceed, Jess tagged along as an observer.

'This is not *Mission: Impossible*,' she told them as they crept past the machine shed. 'It's straightforward breaking and entering. Observe and time the patrol patterns, choose your window and sneak through. Don't all rush in there together. Assign roles and stick to your plan.'

It amused Jess to hear herself. On the one hand, it appeared she had found her calling, but really, she was parroting a script from a Kingdom of Hades handbook downloaded from their website. The organisation's digital security protocols were watertight and ever changing to evade the attention of government agencies, who were underfunded, understaffed and unmotivated. Jess had absorbed the training booklet with a fierce devotion that had, ironically, reminded her of Hayley's descriptions of church doctrine all those years ago. *Finally got religion*, she thought. Hayley had her own creed now, too. Saltless as a substitute for Episcopalian. She already had the foundation. Reversion to proselytising wasn't much of a stretch. Jess thought about her frequently now. Ebony's ninth birthday was fast approaching.

Her team decided to allocate two of their number as lookouts and another as a decoy to draw security away from the post office. The remaining two crouched by a shed packed with rusted machinery, waiting for the guards to abandon their posts and rush into the night in pursuit of the decoy. Jess knew Georgia would have promised them a treat if they caught any of the infiltrators.

Jess accompanied the two team leaders as they dashed across the open ground to the door of the post office. It was padlocked. One of the women, Brooke, glanced at Jess for direction.

'Don't look at me,' Jess whispered.

'Use the freeze spray,' her companion hissed. That was Veda, a fine prospect. Steely-eyed and hungry for revenge, but not blinded by it.

Brooke located the canister in her pack, popped the lid and was about to spray the padlock when Jess intervened.

'Goggles,' she reprimanded her. 'Get that shit in your eye and you'll be in emergency tonight, answering all sorts of uncomfortable questions.'

Brooke and Veda donned their eye protection and Jess stepped back as Brooke sprayed the padlock with white foam.

'Now, wait thirty seconds,' Jess said. 'This is why you need to time an incursion correctly.'

Half a minute passed. Both women looked up at Jess again.

'Well?' she said.

'Stand back,' Veda told Brooke. She stood up and kicked the padlock with the heel of her boot. It fractured and fell away from the door. Veda beamed, her teeth glinting in the moonlight like tombstones.

'Inside, quickly,' Jess told them.

It was pitch black inside the post office. Veda and Brooke clicked on their torches and shone them around the interior.

'Keep those beams pointed at the floor,' Jess growled.

She waited by the counter until the recruits located the cupboard. Brooke acted quickly this time, spraying the smaller padlock. The cupboard was mounted too high on the wall to kick, but Veda cast around until she found a stone paperweight and used that to break the lock instead.

The recruits enjoyed a moment of triumph when they obtained the coffee tin. Their victory was short-lived, however, for when they hastened back to the door, Georgia and two of her security guards were blocking the exit. One of them was Nicky.

'Shit,' Brooke said, throwing up her arms in defeat. Veda looked uncertainly at Jess, who slowly shook her head.

'You going to give up just like that?' Jess asked.

'We're caught,' Brooke said.

'Are you?' Georgia said, stepping aside. 'Security between you and daylight, sure, but there's two of them, and two of you.'

The four recruits exchanged uneasy glances.

'How badly do you want to get out of here?' Jess asked.

Veda's nostrils flared. She tucked the coffee tin under one arm. Jess could see the exact moment her recruit crossed the Rubicon, that instant when Veda realised there were no rules, not anymore. She charged the security guards, striking Nicky in the neck with a flailing elbow while the other woman attempted to restrain her. Veda shoved her assailant in the chest, knocking her to the floor, then bolted out the door, leapt down the steps to the grass in a single bound and sprinted away into the night. Shocked by the sudden act of violence, Brooke hesitated for a moment before apologising to the fallen women and fleeing after her teammate.

Georgia and Jess helped the security guards to their feet, their pride wounded but no real physical damage sustained.

'She punched me in the throat,' Nicky protested.

'Sorry, mate,' Jess said. 'There's going to be some rough-and-tumble from here on in. Next time hit her back.'

'I fucking will,' Nicky said, rubbing her neck.

The incursion was not a complete success. The decoy and both lookouts were captured. Those three women had to spend the night in the cold gloom of the mine. As they were marched to their punishment, Veda fell into step beside Jess.

'Good job,' Jess congratulated her.

'I lost three of my team,' Veda said. 'What could I have done better?'

'You didn't need the lookouts,' Jess told her. 'Too static, and what were they watching for? They had no way of alerting you when security was approaching your position.'

'Should have run three decoys,' Veda said, frustrated.

Jess smiled approvingly.

'Now you're getting it,' she said. 'Sow confusion. Thin their resources.'

Veda nodded, taking note.

'You can handle yourself in a scrape,' Jess commented.

'Grew up with four brothers and two sisters,' Veda said. 'That was nothing.'

They followed a narrow-gauge railway line downhill to the mouth of the mine. The metal gate displayed a faded 'No Entry, Authorised Persons Only' sign. It opened in a squeal of rusted hinges. The rail line vanished into darkness beyond. The three captured women sheepishly filed in, buttressed by encouraging slaps on the back and wellwishing from their fellow recruits. Georgia swung the gate closed behind them.

'Stay near the entrance,' she said. 'I don't want to have to winch any of your corpses out of a shaft because you decided to go exploring. There's a bucket to piss in, and a couple of blankets. We'll come get you in the morning.'

'Yeah, I'll bring you an espresso, bitches,' Veda said, laughing.

The rest of the recruits dispersed, returning to their cottages for the night. As winner of the evening's manoeuvres, Veda walked in tandem with Jess and Georgia.

'You feeling it, mate?' Jess asked her.

'Fucking oath,' Veda said. 'What a rush. Can't wait to get out there and cause some mayhem.'

'Just remember why we're doing this,' Jess said. 'We're not anarchists, disrupting the dominant paradigm for fun.'

Veda's jaw stiffened. 'I know why I'm here,' she said. 'They sat back and let my daughter die.'

'Who did?' Jess asked, fishing for the correct answer.

'The Decadians,' Veda said, spitting on the grass. 'Politicians and rich elites whose children were lucky enough to miss the cut-off. They're behind this. No question. They want us to forget what happened, to move on. They won't get away with it that easily.'

'Word, sister,' Georgia said. 'They will know our suffering.'

The trio walked in silence until they came to Jess and Georgia's cottage.

'Where'd you learn that trick with the freeze spray?' Veda asked.

'My husband Steve,' Jess told her. 'He used it at work when engine components were fused and the only way to prise them apart was to break them.'

Veda was impressed. 'This is all new to me,' she said. 'Are there no men in Hades? There are just as many bereaved fathers out there, surely.'

'The blokes have their own splinter groups,' Georgia explained. 'They're not as active in disruption.'

'Men have a different relationship with grief,' Jess said. 'For us, it's like a crow perching on the windowsill every morning, reminding us of the darkness. With them, it's more of a temporary state. They push it down as far as it will go and then tell everyone that they're fine.'

Veda nodded. 'Only for it to destroy them years later. Yeah, my dad was like that when one of my brothers was killed in a hit-and-run. Cried for a month and then that was it, back to the grind, let's never talk of this again.'

'How'd that work out for him?' Georgia asked.

'Pancreatic cancer at fifty-seven.'

Jess stared at the overgrown garden next to the miner's cottage. The bottlebrush was in full bloom.

'Men treat having kids like planting seeds,' she said. 'The seed grows into this little alien thing that's entirely separate from them. They like having it around, but it's abstract. Whereas for us, children are like organs. They're pulsing, beating, living parts of our bodies that sprout arms and legs and walk and cry and break our hearts. They are bound to us in ways no man can ever match or comprehend. They are us, and we are them. That's why it hurts so much when we lose a child. We lose the best part of ourselves.'

Georgia placed a hand on her chest.

'Pippa,' she said.

Veda did the same.

'Gitanjali.'

A tornado was forming in Jess's mind. She shook her head, fighting to clear it.

'Tyler,' she said, feeling her own heartbeat through her jacket.

Veda said goodnight and retired to her cottage, and Georgia and Jess entered their own tiny house. Schnitzel came waddling over to greet them. Baz Luhrmann remained by the fireplace, snoring. The fire was down to embers, so Georgia added a few logs. Within minutes, the wood was crackling and flames licked the grate.

'You want a cuppa?' she asked Jess. 'I can put on the billy.'

'Sure,' Jess said. 'Do we have any ginger and lemon left?'

'Think there's still a few bags,' Georgia said.

Jess fetched the tea bags from the minuscule kitchen and popped them into mugs. She marvelled at how a family of six had once lived in such a cramped space.

'You believe that rhetoric about Decadian elites?' Georgia asked as she poured boiling water into the cups.

'Don't you?' Jess asked, surprised.

'Kinda,' Georgia said. 'I find it hard to relate, out here in the country. The closest we have is that prick Van der Saar.' Georgia glanced at Jess as she blew on her tea. 'You and he were an item for a while, eh?'

'Long time ago, when we were kids,' Jess said. 'And then again, briefly, about ten years back.'

Georgia raised an eyebrow.

'Seriously?' she said.

'Just a one-night stand,' Jess said, smiling faintly at the memory. 'It was my birthday. I wanted to treat myself.'

Georgia's eyes narrowed as she assessed her comrade in arms.

'That's not going to interfere with our plans, is it?'

'On the contrary,' Jess told her, tentatively sipping the hot tea. 'You're right. He's an entitled bastard. Always has been. I'm sick of him trying to galvanise the community and pull everyone together for the common good.'

'For his good.'

'Exactly,' Jess said. 'Next thing he'll be running for mayor.'

'Not without his legs,' Georgia said.

'We need to make a statement,' Jess said, pounding her fist on the table. 'Stay the course and show them we will not be ignored, no matter the cost.'

The two women instinctively ducked when something landed on the cottage roof. They froze, listening for a moment as clawed feet scrabbled across the tin. Schnitzel's tail shot up and she watched the ceiling, head dipped to one side in concentration. Beside her on the mat, Baz Luhrmann did not stir. One back leg and the corner of his jowls twitched, but his deep sleep was uninterrupted by possum claws.

* * *

THE SENSOR LIGHT BY THE ENTRANCE TO THE SCRAPYARD flickered into life when the Doberman pinscher loped to the gate and sniffed the air. A car passed on the highway, the beam of its headlights briefly revealing a green Ford Falcon parked beneath a Moreton Bay fig. The tree's branches intertwined with the three-metre-high wire mesh fence surrounding the yard, providing a passageway for nocturnal marsupials to the rusted school bus in the corner of the depot. The vehicle no longer had any wheels and was supported by cement breeze blocks.

Jess timed how long it took for the sensor light to switch off after the Doberman returned to its kennel.

'Sixty seconds,' she told Georgia when the yard was plunged back into darkness. She stopped the chronograph on her watch and reset it to zero.

'We'll need to throw the meat out of sensor range,' Georgia said.

'Won't matter,' Jess said, unwrapping the piece of sirloin on her lap. 'There's enough tranquilliser in this to drop a horse. As long as he goes back to bed after eating it, he'll be out for the rest of the night.'

'All right, I'll keep watch while you chuck it over the fence.'

The two women got out of the car and calmly walked to the base of the fig tree. The dog heard them and came charging through the yard, barking his warning. Georgia stepped back at the sight of his slobbering jaws, but Jess made soothing sounds and waved the cut of meat in the air. The dog stopped barking and tilted his head. Jess could tell he was interested in what she had to offer. Rather than attempt to throw it over the mesh fence and risk the steak landing on the roof of the bus, Jess held the meat up to a gap in the wire. The dog sniffed at it, then gently took the sirloin in his mouth, pulled it through the mesh and padded happily back to his kennel.

'Now we wait,' Jess said.

'How long do you reckon?' Georgia asked.

'Twenty minutes and we should be good to go.'

'Mind if I smoke?'

Jess indicated that they should shelter in the lee of the tree to avoid detection from the road. The scrapyard abutted the highway to Langdale, ten kilometres outside Gattan. There was no reason for anyone to go there at night. Georgia lit a cigarette and cupped the glowing tip in her palm.

'Just as well we left the mutts at the cottage,' she said. 'Schnitzel would have barked up a storm. Baz, not so much. Friendly fella, eh? I'm not used to big dogs, but he's all right.'

'He brought me a caterpillar one time,' Jess said, leaning against the trunk. 'Didn't hurt it, just dropped it at my feet as if he was saying, *hey, look what I found.*'

'I got Schnitz for Pippa after Danny pissed off,' Georgia said. 'Schnitz was so upset when we found her. Wouldn't stop barking. She knew Pippa was gone. Pined for months after. I still find her sleeping in Pip's room sometimes.'

'Did you keep her room as it was?' Jess asked gently.

'Yeah. I know I shouldn't. The psychologist said it's counterintuitive to the grieving process but, you know, fuck her.'

'I preserved Tyler's room at first,' Jess admitted. 'But it was wrecking me. After I joined Hades, I packed everything into boxes and donated it to the Salvos.'

'Wow,' Georgia said. 'I couldn't.'

'Don't get me wrong, I kept a few mementos, but it was starting to creep me out, seeing his clothes in the drawers. I figured that I didn't need his stuff to remember him. Also, the doctor said I should do it for Steve's mental health.'

'Steve working again?' Georgia asked.

'Three days a week, when the power's on,' Jess confirmed. 'Gets him out of the house and out of my hair. Spends the rest of his time in the pub or taking Baz for long walks. I hardly see him. We have separate lives now. Suits me.'

'Danny and I split up years back,' Georgia said. 'He was never home anyway. Worked the rigs out west. The money was good, but he'd spend it on dumb shit. Boys' toys. Drones, fancy watches, a jetski. He drove a ute that cost ninety grand. Said he liked the sound and the colour.'

'Big babies, aren't they?' Jess said. 'He still in WA?'

'No, he died,' Georgia said matter-of-factly.

'Sorry, mate, I didn't know,' Jess told her.

'It was a while ago, after the separation. Pippa was only four at the time, so she didn't really remember him.' Georgia drew deeply on her cigarette. 'He drowned during a storm. Cable snapped and he was washed off the platform. His body was never recovered.'

'That's rough,' Jess said.

Georgia shrugged. 'At least I had Pip. She was the best kid. So smart and funny. I was constantly in awe of her. Like, how did that come out of me? She was a fluke. One in a million.' Georgia exhaled a plume of smoke and closed her eyes, remembering. 'Six weeks away from her tenth birthday. Mother*fucker*. It was just me and her at home. I had no idea what was happening. And that fucking creepy Latin chanting. I still hear it, echoing around in my brain when I'm trying to sleep.'

'The ballad of Orpheus,' Jess said. 'The most beautiful voice of antiquity. His songs made the gods weep.'

'You believe all that, don't you?'

'Sure, why not?' Jess shrugged. 'After hearing him sing, Hades agreed to release his wife from the underworld, if he walked in front of her and didn't look back.'

'Yeah, like he was auditioning for *Greek Idol*,' Georgia said. 'I prefer the story about his severed head being encased in a shrine on Lesbos. You know that was destroyed? Half the island blown to pieces.'

'The cycle of nine continues,' Jess said. 'It won't stop, and neither will we.'

They fell into silence then, listening to the sounds of the night as they waited for the tranquilliser to take effect.

'It's gone very quiet back there,' Georgia said, peering through the fence.

'That's long enough,' Jess said, checking her watch. She opened the back door of the Falcon and grabbed a set of bolt cutters. They had decided it would be less intrusive to enter the yard via a hole in the mesh, rather than break the padlock on the main gate. Jess was also concerned about video surveillance at the entrance. She painstakingly cut a section of mesh close to the school bus, enough for them to bend back the wire and slip through.

Once they were inside the fence, they hugged the side of the bus and crept past a stack of old cars until they were out of range of the movement sensor. Jess switched on her torch and pointed it at the dog kennel. The Doberman was lying on its side, tongue lolling. She moved closer to confirm the dog was sleeping, not dead. She crouched by the kennel and stroked the Doberman's flank before examining the name tag attached to its collar.

'Drogon,' she told Georgia, laughing.

'One of Khaleesi's dragons,' Georgia said. 'Hope there aren't two more lurking in the shadows.'

'If you hear someone saying *dracarys*, run,' Jess said.

'The loot is under that awning,' Georgia said, shining her torch at the back of the main shed. Leaving Drogon to dream of immolating priests, the two women carefully navigated a maze of rusted farm machinery until they came to a stack of paint tins full of old screws and nails. Jess lifted a tin down from the pile.

'Oof,' she said, placing it on the ground. 'That must weigh ten kilos.'

'How many do we need?' Georgia asked, surveying the stack.

'Couple of dozen, I reckon.'

'So, like, thirty?' Georgia said, dubious. 'That's three hundred kilos, Jess. We should have brought the van. The suspension on the Falcon is fucked as it is.'

'Let's see how many we can take,' she said. 'I'll settle for twenty.'

So began the arduous task of carrying the heavy tins of nails across the yard to the gap in the fence. They stacked the tins on the soft earth below the fig tree. After their second trip, Georgia returned to the car to fetch a pair of gardening gloves. Jess found a stiff pair of her own draped across the handle of a wheelbarrow parked by the tin shed.

It took fifteen minutes to liberate twenty-two tins of nails. They only activated the motion sensor twice during their travails, and on each occasion made sure they halted in the shadows until the light was extinguished again. Drogon snored contentedly throughout.

Once the task was complete, Jess bent the mesh back into place and rested against the tree. Georgia was slumped on the ground, her breathing shallow.

'I need to quit the smokes,' she said.

'Come on, let's get them loaded,' Jess said.

Georgia hauled herself to her feet and opened the boot of the car, shoving some detritus out of the way to make room for the tins. Jess handed them to her, one at a time, and Georgia arranged them in rows until the boot was full. She stepped back to assess the suspension. The rear of the Falcon was hanging low over the wheels.

'Go slow, and try not to hit any potholes,' Jess told her.

'What's our story if we get pulled over?' Georgia asked.

'Not going to happen,' Jess said. 'I haven't seen a copper in weeks.'

'I'll stick to eighty until we reach town. That dirt road into the mine might be an issue.'

Jess nodded and climbed into the passenger seat. Georgia started the engine and rolled the Falcon down the incline to the hard shoulder of the highway. She pulled out slowly and crossed the median strip to the other side of the road.

'She's really dragging,' she said.

'Wrong vehicle,' Jess agreed. 'Sorry, mate. We'll know for next time. I didn't think they'd be so heavy.'

'Should've just sent Nicky to buy them.'

'Nah, that would only raise suspicion,' Jess said. 'Who buys two dozen tins of rusty nails?'

'Fair point.'

They encountered no vehicles during the short, ponderous drive into Gattan. Rather than go through the centre of town, Georgia pulled onto a back road that wound a circuitous route through the housing estate. They emerged on the far side of town, turning back onto the main artery for a few hundred metres before taking the gravel road that led to the mine. Georgia slowed to a crawl at that point, concerned that a strut or ball joint would snap under the extreme weight.

There were no candles burning in any of the miner's cottages when they arrived, although wisps of wood smoke curled from two of the chimneys. Georgia drove directly to the mouth of the mine and reversed the Falcon down the incline as far as she dared.

She and Jess worked fast, unloading the tins of nails. Once they were done, Georgia drove the car back up the hill to level ground.

'She's on her last legs, that old girl,' she said when she returned.

'Her sacrifice won't be in vain,' Jess said.

Georgia swung open the gate to the mine and switched on her torch. The beam of light was swallowed as the shaft stretched back into absolute darkness. Jess carried one of the tins inside and placed it by the entrance. She then activated her own torch and placed it on the tin, angling the beam so she and

Georgia could see where they were going. The torch illuminated the array of supplies that had been surreptitiously gathered by recruits during the training camp. Everything on the list Jess had dictated to Nicky was now present.

Six fifty-litre barrels of ammonium nitrate were pushed up against the rock wall. Those would be used as fuel for the main bomb. Jess and Georgia wearily carried all twenty-two tins of nails into the cavern, stacking them next to a dozen jars of ethylene. The sharp projectiles would find their way back inside Georgia's Ford Falcon again one day soon, as the main ingredient in a secondary explosive device that would lay waste to civilians fleeing the site of the primary detonation. This was standard procedure in the Kingdom of Hades downloadable handbook: wreak the maximum amount of carnage. It had proved an effective technique in more than thirty countries around the globe. None were exempt from the siren song beckoning the dead into the underworld. None would be spared – especially those who defied the will of the gods.

Jess and Georgia brushed themselves down and congratulated themselves on a successful night's work. As they turned to leave, neither of them noticed that one of the captured women from the coffee-tin exercise had utilised her time in the temporary prison to proudly carve a trident symbol into the rockface.

PART EIGHT

PEPPR

A TAWNY FROGMOUTH SWOOPED DOWN AND LANDED AWKWARDLY on the lawn of the nursing home. Hayley was standing so still, lost in her thoughts, that the bird presumed she was a piece of statuary, like the giant Buddha head the owners of Rose Grove had installed in the garden to give the residents something to look at. The bird had a small creature in its talons – a mouse, maybe, or a baby possum. A big catch for a frogmouth – they usually ate snails and worms.

Hayley watched as the bird used its beak to slice into the belly of its prey, guts spilling out onto the freshly cut grass. As it consumed the catch, the tawny made a satisfied *ooohm ooohm ooohm ooohm* sound, like the subdued bassline to a techno track.

Hayley flashed to the bush rave she and Jude had attended when Ebony was six, held on private land in the hills beyond Mount Darling. Irresponsible parenting, maybe, but they'd taken mushrooms and danced to relentless psychedelic trance music until their quadriceps ached. Ebony had loved it. She ran around with a bunch of other feral kids up way past their usual bedtime, then crashed in the tent next to her exhausted mothers, the trio falling asleep in a tangle of sleeping bags as a bass thrum reverberated in the marrow of their bones.

Hayley snapped out of her stupor and moved towards the entrance of the care facility. She had been doing that lately, halting at random moments as if on pause. Jude had insisted she see their doctor about the phenomenon she referred to as 'waking blackouts', but the physician offered no diagnosis other than to suggest the incidents might be a form of paralysis stemming from the persistent dread of the inevitable.

The receptionist buzzed her through the entry and Hayley signed in at the desk. When she opened the door to room thirty-eight, she found her mother sitting in a comfortable chair by the window, staring vacantly at the garden beyond. Penny was a gaunt shadow of her former self, her cheeks sunken and her arms so thin they were almost skeletal, but she still looked up and smiled when her daughter entered, bearing a posy of irises.

'Hello, Mum,' Hayley said, bending down to kiss her mother on the cheek.

'Oh, these are lovely,' Penny said. 'I'll put them in water.'

'Don't get up, I'll do it,' Hayley said. The vase on the side table was empty. Hayley frowned, wondering what had happened to the gerberas she'd brought the previous week. She filled the vase with water and arranged the irises.

'It's a beautiful day,' Penny said.

'Maybe we'll go for a little walk,' Hayley suggested.

Penny nodded enthusiastically. 'Yes, it's time for me to go home.'

Hayley sat in the chair opposite her mother, pulling it close so she could grasp Penny's bony hands. She ignored her mother's comment. She knew from experience that it was easier to move on to another topic than to explain for the thousandth time that Penny lived here now.

'How have you been?' Hayley asked. 'Sorry I haven't visited. It's been a difficult week. Jude and I had another big fight.'

Penny was momentarily concerned, but then patted the back of her daughter's hand. 'Marriage is hard,' she said, chuckling. 'Ask your father. He and I have our fair share of disagreements. Is he parking the car? He always likes to get a good spot.'

Hayley licked her lips as she considered her options. Joseph Carlisle had dropped dead from a heart attack in the local IGA five years prior. He fell headfirst into a display of fabric softener. Blue liquid oozed from under his twitching body, as if it were leaking from his arteries. Her father passed away while lying face down on the tiles with the scent of Cuddly hypoallergenic sunshine fresh wafting through his nostrils.

'Dad's not coming today,' Hayley said. It was easier that way. 'He had to go to Bunnings and pick up some planters.' The more elaborate the lie, the easier it was to sell.

'Yes, it's that time of year, isn't it?' Penny said. 'That's fine, he can pick me up later.'

The thought of Penny outliving Ebony horrified Hayley, firstly because it was against the laws of nature that a grandparent should survive their grandchild, but also because Hayley dreaded the prospect of continuing to visit her mother and having to explain, over and over, where Ebony was, and the disaster that had befallen the world. Where would she even begin? She'd just that morning read an article about Kingdom of Hades' inane belief in something called the cycle of nine. Madness reigned supreme. Society was on the verge of collapse, as every child under nine was doomed to an early grave.

She had tried eliminating salt from her daughter's diet, but so had millions of others and that hadn't prevented their children from bursting into song and then perishing in abject terror. Hayley couldn't bear having to relive the trauma every time she visited her mother, who had been rendered a shell of her former self by the dementia. Explaining the frequent power outages was difficult enough. Her mother had largely been insulated from society's decline in fortunes. Hayley sometimes felt a little envious of that.

'And how's work going?' Penny asked.

Hayley took a deep breath before launching into the familiar explanation.

'My business closed a while ago, Mum,' she said. Ingredients for Hayley's Freelance bars became too difficult to source, not to mention horrendously expensive. 'We live on Jude's salary now. She's still employed, although we don't know for how much longer. The state government are going through, umm, a period of transition.'

'What about those videos you showed me on your phone?' Penny asked. 'I thought you were a celebrity chef.'

'Hardly,' Hayley said, and continued with the more inconvenient truth. 'Maybe for a minute, but there was no money in it. I deleted my social media accounts. Those platforms became toxic. It wasn't good for my mental health being on Instagram all the time.'

This did not seem to register with Penny. She looked past Hayley, straining to see if anyone else was in the room. Hayley sighed, aware that these visits were largely spent talking to herself. She didn't mind. She found the sessions relaxing.

'What are you looking for, Mum? Do you need something?'

'No, silly me, I thought Ebony might be here but of course she'd be in school.'

Yet another thing to explain or lie about. Hayley decided to be truthful in this regard.

'Actually, she's at home,' she said. 'She doesn't get out much.'

'Nonsense,' Penny said. 'A healthy young girl like that should be running around enjoying nature on a glorious day like this.'

'That's what Jude says too,' Hayley sniffed. 'I tend to disagree.'

'For goodness sake, Hayley, don't be such a stick in the mud,' Penny said, rapping her daughter across the knuckles. 'You should be more open-minded. Let the girl live a little.'

Hayley shook her head in disbelief.

'That's rich, coming from you,' she said, struggling to hold her temper in check.

'When's your father getting here?' Penny abruptly changed tack. 'We're going to be late for church.'

Hayley released her mother's hand and leant back in the chair.

'You'll be pleased to hear I've been going again,' she confessed.

That, at least, wasn't a lie. Hayley had unexpectedly found solace in faith. If that surprised her, she took comfort in the fact she wasn't the only one. Church attendance had skyrocketed. Everyone was desperate.

'Oh, that's wonderful,' Penny said, clasping her palms together. 'God is our refuge and strength, an ever-present help in trouble.'

'Psalm forty-six,' Hayley said, astonished that her mother could quote Bible verses she'd learnt during childhood yet not recall what she did yesterday.

'Pray with me,' Penny said, extending her hands.

Hayley slipped from the chair onto her knees and grasped her frail mother's papery palms in hers. The elderly woman closed her eyes and bowed her head. Hayley kept her own eyes open, staring out at the lawn, so well tended you wouldn't think a pervading sense of doom lay heavy on everyone's shoulders.

'Therefore we will not fear, though the earth give way and the mountains fall into the heart of the sea, though its waters roar and foam and the mountains quake with their surging,' Hayley said with solemnity, hoping to find solace in the words, thinking of Ebony. 'There is a river whose streams make glad the city of God, the holy place where the Most High dwells. God is within her, she will not fall; God will help her at break of day. Nations are in uproar, kingdoms fall; he lifts his voice, the earth melts.'

* * *

WHEN HAYLEY GOT HOME, EBONY WAS SITTING UP ON HER BED next to Jude, who was explaining long division to their perplexed daughter. Hayley left them to it and went to check emails on her laptop. One was a credit card bill. It didn't matter that the planet was on the brink of chaos, the bills kept coming. Hayley opened the attachment and scrolled down through the items, out of habit. She was disturbed to find dozens of micro-transactions conducted through an app called Peppr. Not recognising the application, she googled it and felt her stomach flip. She closed the laptop and stormed into Ebony's room.

'Phone and iPad, hand them over,' she demanded, clicking her fingers.

'What's going on?' Jude asked.

'Do you know about Peppr?'

'I thought it was salt that concerned us,' Jude said, confused.

'No, the app,' Hayley said, glaring at Ebony, who bore the telltale expression of someone who'd been caught with their hand in the cookie jar. Jude shrugged, baffled.

'You want to explain?' Hayley asked her daughter.

Ebony squirmed. 'It's just a way for me to make friends.'

Jude was suspicious now.

'What kind of friends?' she asked. 'Ebony, we've talked about this. It's not safe chatting with strangers online. They could be anyone.'

'No, it's only for girls like me,' she protested.

Jude looked quizzically at Hayley.

'Dozens of micro transactions on my Mastercard,' she explained. 'I looked it up. Peppr is a messaging app for saltless kids looking to rebel against their overbearing parents. It's all over the forums. They get advice on how to evade holistic saltless practices and can even order salted treats through in-app purchases.'

'Who's behind it?' Jude said, alarmed.

'Good question,' Hayley said. 'Big Salt, maybe.'

'Let's not start that again.'

Ebony quickly locked her iPad and folded her arms in defiance.

'I'm not allowed to do anything,' she said.

'It's for your own good,' Hayley said. 'Devices, now.'

Ebony threw the iPad down on the bed and collected her phone from the charging pad, handing that over, too.

'What's your passcode?' Hayley asked her.

'Not telling.'

'Open it, *now*,' Hayley said, holding out the phone. Jude observed, jaw clenched.

'No,' Ebony said.

'Ebony Hay-Jude Carlisle-Tan, you are in so much trouble right now,' Hayley said. She only ever reverted to Ebony's full name when she was furious. Ebony hated the hyphenation and didn't appreciate the Beatles reference. She preferred Taylor Swift.

Ebony shook her head in point-blank refusal.

Hayley suddenly grabbed her daughter by the hair and held her face to the phone screen. Ebony squealed and tried to pull away, and Hayley gripped tighter. The girl yelped in pain and began to cry.

'Babe, stop it,' Jude said. 'Let her go.'

Hayley persisted until the home screen appeared, then she shoved her daughter back onto the pillow. Jude reached across the bed and grabbed his wife by the wrist.

'Hurt her again and I'll—'

'You'll what?' Hayley said. 'Go on, tell me.'

'Don't put me in that position,' Jude said.

Hayley pulled her arm away and tapped the pepper pot icon on the screen. She scanned through the menus in the app.

'It's full of discussion threads and recipes and articles like "Unfair Saltless Parenting" and "Nine Secret Salty Treats",' she said, before covering her mouth in shock. 'There's a section on how to prepare for death. Bucket lists of things they should try to experience. Prayers to ancient gods.'

'Fuck,' Jude said, taking the phone from Hayley's shaking hand. She scrolled through the app. 'This sounds like Kingdom of Hades.'

Hayley slumped onto the bed. Behind her, Ebony had buried her face in the pillow and was sobbing uncontrollably. Hayley rubbed her back.

'I'm sorry I was stern with you before,' she said. 'But you mustn't listen to these people, Eb. They're dangerous. They want everyone to suffer just like they have.'

Ebony sat up and wiped her eyes.

'I don't want to die in this room,' she said.

'You're not going to die here or anywhere else,' Hayley said, stroking her cheek.

'I am, Mum,' she said. 'Just like everyone else.'

'I won't accept that,' Hayley said. 'We're not giving up.'

Hayley and Jude sat either side of their daughter, hugging her until she stopped crying. To Hayley's surprise, Jude handed Ebony the phone.

'No more spending money in the app,' she said. 'And let me or Mum see your chats from now on. Too many perverts and weirdos out there, Eb.'

Ebony nodded and gratefully accepted her devices. Hayley beckoned for Jude to follow her out to the kitchen.

'Just like that, you give them back to her?' she said, turning on her partner.

'She doesn't have much time left,' Jude said.

'And you throw her into the arms of those maniacs?'

'No, she uses it to chat with other saltless kids. She's imprisoned here, Hayles. It's not much of a life, given these are probably her final weeks.'

'Now you're on their side?'

'Whose side?' Jude said, becoming increasingly frustrated. 'I'm not on anyone's side. I'm on our side. I'll do everything I can to save our girl, but she still has a right to live while she's here. Do you want her last words to be that she hates you?'

'I want her to listen to us,' Hayley said. 'We're her parents. She's only eight. We know what's best for her.'

'You sound like your mother.'

'That's not fair,' Hayley said, and, in an instant, she was back in her childhood bedroom, patiently enduring a lecture from her mum about the lack of moral fibre in her schoolfriends, especially that trollop Jessica Ward. Penny claimed Jess's errant ways could be explained by an absence of devotional purpose. If only she could accept God into her life, then she would attain clarity and direction. At the time Hayley had groaned, rolled her eyes and waited for the sermon to end, but now she wasn't so sure. Hayley needed something to cling to, a promise of better days to come, a sliver of hope that her daughter would be the exception to this universal rule, that they wouldn't hear those words – *Lascivi pueri ad muscas deis sumus, Nos ad ludibrium necant* – come out of her mouth ever. Perhaps if she prayed harder, there would be salvation. It was worth a shot. Ebony only had a few weeks left. She would try anything.

Jude's clicking fingers snapped Hayley out of her torpor.

'Hello, anyone in there?' Jude said. 'You did it again, babe. You were off in your own private world.'

Hayley blinked repeatedly, suddenly deafened by an incessant, otherworldly hum. Jude's voice faded into the background as Hayley was abruptly transported seven years into the past. She was sitting on the lounge-room rug, watching Ebony as she chewed on a blue dinosaur plushie. The toy was soaked through. Hayley hadn't spoken to an adult all day. It was just her and the baby, locked in a staring contest while *The Wiggles* played on the iPad. Hayley hated them already. She resented the fact she knew the lyrics to their songs. She wiped Ebony's mouth for the umpteenth time and thought about the other parents she'd met at kindy. Hayley had nothing in common with those people, other than a bawling infant. Would they be her friends now? Was this her life? She rocked back and forth on the rug, mimicking her little girl. *Hold it together*, she thought. *Hold on.*

When awareness of her surroundings returned, Hayley was standing alone in the kitchen, her ears ringing.

* * *

EVEN THOUGH SHE WASN'T SUPPOSED TO GO THERE, EBONY wanted to see Chambers Street before she died. She stuck to the footpath most of the way, elated to be out of the house at all. Jude had pumped up the tyres on her bike and told her she could meet her Peppr pals if she was home within ninety minutes. Hayley was attending a slow flow yoga class in Rushglen and wouldn't be back for hours. Ebony jumped at the chance for freedom, however brief.

The fire that began at 17 Chambers Street had consumed four houses before the CFA managed to get it under control. A local council member and his family died from smoke inhalation. The remaining residents escaped unhurt. It was assumed the blaze had been started maliciously, but no one claimed responsibility and no arrests were made.

Ebony halted in front of the blackened shell of number seventeen and took a photo with her phone. There was a message thread about the fire on Peppr. She uploaded the image to the thread and wrote: *Spooky!* Someone claimed the councillor and his kids were murdered because he opposed a grant for an Orphean family. Someone else said he started the fire himself because he didn't want his kids to swell up and die when they turned nine. Ebony didn't know what to think. She'd read on the message boards that some kids her age took pills and went to sleep forever or jumped off a cliff into the sea and drowned rather than face the morning of their ninth birthday. Or their parents took them to a faraway place, and they never returned. Ebony found it hard to believe it was going to happen to her soon.

She put her phone away and rode further along Chambers Street, passing the scorched houses before turning down behind the nursing home where her grandmother lived and crossing to the playground on the other side of the street. Three other kids she knew from Peppr were waiting for her: Xavier, Willow and Harvey. Ebony knew them from school, but it had been a while since they'd met in person. She parked her bike next to theirs and joined Willow on the swings, waving hello to Xavier and Harvey, who shoved each other out of the way to be first down the slide.

Willow offered her a sour worm lolly.

'Do they have salt?' Ebony asked.

Willow consulted the ingredients, then shrugged.

'They don't taste salty,' she said.

'I don't care, anyway,' Ebony said, taking two of the sour worms and biting one in half.

'Did you sneak out?' Willow asked.

'Nope,' Ebony said. 'Mum let me go. My nice mum.'

'My big brother unlocked a window for me,' Willow said. 'He's going to be in so much trouble when Dad finds out, but he says he'll deal with it.'

'I have an older sister,' Ebony said, kicking her feet high in the air. 'Sort of. Half-sister. We both have the same dad. She lives with him. It's meant to be a secret, but everybody knows.'

'My dad says we're catching a boat to Tasmania before my birthday. We're going to climb a mountain or something.'

Bored with the slide, Xavier and Harvey sidled over to pester the girls. Harvey grabbed Ebony's swing, causing her to pinwheel awkwardly from side to side. She shrieked and laughed.

'Stop it!'

'Hurry up,' he said. 'I want a go.'

Willow offered the boys lollies, and Xavier immediately dug his fist into the packet and grabbed a handful.

'Hey, one each!' Willow said.

Ignoring her, Xavier stuffed three in his mouth at once.

'I'm not supposed to have these,' Harvey said, turning the gummy worm over in his hand. Eventually he reneged and took a bite, eyelids fluttering in ecstasy.

'What else are you not allowed to do?' Ebony asked him.

'Hardly anything,' Harvey said. 'Mum and Dad won't let me have burgers, or peanut butter or nothing.'

'I have ten dollars,' Xavier said. 'We could go to Macca's now and get cheeseburgers.'

Harvey shook his head sadly.

'It's not Macca's anymore,' he said. 'Danny Murphy's mum and dad took it over after McDonald's moved out. They even painted the big M green. My photo's on their Saltless board. They're not allowed to serve me.'

'I'll get us something salty,' Xavier promised.

'It's okay, I'm not bothered,' Harvey said, sitting on the swing when Ebony vacated it for him. 'Don't really like it anyway. When you haven't had salt for a while, the taste is like woah!'

'It's not like it makes a difference,' Willow said. 'We're still going to die.'

The four children kicked their heels in the tanbark. Willow gave everyone another gummy worm to cheer them up.

'How long do you have left?' Ebony asked her.

'Five and a bit weeks. You're going sooner, eh?'

Ebony nodded. 'Two weeks today.'

'I still have four months,' Xavier said.

'I have a countdown on my iPad,' Harvey told them. 'Eighty-seven days before I burst.' He puffed out his cheeks and made an explosion sound.

'On Peppr, they say it really hurts,' Xavier said.

Willow dismissed this. 'No, doctors give you an injection just before your time, so you don't feel anything.'

'Are you going to sing the song?' Harvey asked. 'I already know the words. I've been practising.'

'You don't need to know them,' Ebony said. 'They just come out of you.'

'It's the voice of some old god from Greece speaking through you,' Xavier said. 'That's what it says on Peppr, anyway.'

'Rubbish,' Willow told him. 'My dad says it's aliens doing it.'

'Cool,' Harvey said. 'I hope they take us up into space.'

'My mum says I'll go to heaven,' Ebony offered. 'That's a bit like space.'

'See you there, I guess,' Willow said, jumping off the swing at full tilt. She landed in a crouch and stood up, taking a bow while the others clapped.

'Let's go on the roundabout,' Xavier proposed.

All four children jumped on the roundabout, grabbing a handle while pushing furiously at the ground to set the ride in motion. Xavier kept pedalling while the others spun, making the wheel turn faster and faster until they were all gripping the bars intensely. He tried to jump off before the ride slowed and sprawled into the tanbark. Ebony, Willow and Harvey laughed uproariously as Xavier brushed himself down, dazed.

'I wish I could meet Lionel Messi before it happens to me,' Harvey said as the roundabout ground to a halt.

'As if,' Xavier told him.

'My dad's taking us all to Dreamworld for Christmas,' Willow said.

'I thought you were going to Tasmania?' Ebony asked.

'We're doing that after.'

'Sounds like a pretty good summer,' Xavier ventured.

'Yeah, apart from the dying bit.' Willow crossed her eyes and stuck her tongue out the corner of her mouth.

'Maybe I'll ask Mum and Dad to take me to Dreamworld,' Harvey said, stroking his chin in contemplation.

'Ask for something bigger,' Xavier advised him. 'What about Disneyland?'

'That's in America,' Ebony said.

'So?' Xavier said.

'There's like a war going on over there,' Willow told him.

'No point, anyway,' Harvey said. 'I saw on Peppr that they've banned eight-year-olds. They don't want anyone blowing up on a ride.'

'You ever seen someone pop?' Xavier asked.

'I have,' Ebony ventured. 'I was at the oval when it first happened.'

'You were there?' Willow asked, impressed.

'Was there, like, blood everywhere and stuff?' Harvey asked.

'Yep,' Ebony said, unsettled by the images that she had tried so hard to forget. 'Coming out of their mouths and their eyes and . . . other places.'

Xavier shook his head. 'No, thank you. I'm taking that injection when the time comes.'

The group fell silent for a moment as the children considered the terrible fate that awaited them.

'I know something cool we could do,' Harvey said. The others leant in eagerly. 'I've always wanted to check out the abandoned mine, but I've never been allowed to go.'

'My big brother went with his friends one time,' Willow said, clearly excited at the prospect of entering forbidden territory.

'I don't know,' Ebony said cautiously. 'Isn't it dangerous?'

'Scared you might die?' Xavier asked her.

'I'd rather fall into a bottomless pit than swell up and burst,' Harvey said.

'You only have two weeks left,' Willow said. 'What does it matter?'

'I suppose,' Ebony said. 'It's just, I didn't think I was going to die *today*, that's all. I'm not even wearing my favourite shoes.'

Harvey and Xavier mounted their bikes. Willow picked hers up and stood next to them. Reluctantly, Ebony joined the group. She knew that by the time they rode to the mine and back, her mum would be home from yoga, and that she would have to endure her wrath. Then she realised Willow was right. It didn't matter. Nothing did.

The four riders kept to the back streets of Gattan to avoid detection. The houses thinned as they neared the mine, and the properties became more dilapidated. Tyre swings and faded Australian flags hung from gum trees in front yards. Rusted cars that hadn't moved in years were parked on nature strips, long grass enshrouding their wheels as nature tried to absorb the forgotten vehicles. Crates of free lemons rotted at the ends of driveways. The bitumen turned to gravel, and then to packed dirt littered with potholes. Dogs barked as the cyclists passed. Magpies observed curiously from powerlines.

An aluminium gate blocked the entrance to the mine site, and a semicircular furrow in the earth indicated that it had recently been dragged shut. That did not deter the children, who bypassed the gate with ease, clambering over it and passing their bikes across to their friends.

The mine was deserted, as they had expected it to be. Harvey led the way, boldly riding to the old visitor centre and dismounting.

'Leave the bikes,' he said. 'We can squeeze through here.'

He indicated an overgrown passageway where the tea-tree had merged with the building. Excited by the prospect of adventure, Ebony dumped her bike and followed Harvey as he ducked under the branches and pushed his way through the scrub.

Once all four children were inside the complex, they stuck to the faint pathways that led to the buildings. Their first port of call was the miner's cottages, abandoned to the ravages of time but still standing, weatherbeaten and sturdy. Ebony and Harvey entered one cottage while Xavier and Willow explored another.

'Someone's been living here,' Ebony said, noticing signs of recent habitation. Old furniture had been pushed against the walls to make room for modern camp beds. The stove and sink were clean, in contrast to the other dusty surfaces. There was freshly chopped wood in the coal bucket by the fire, and ashes in the grate.

'Probably deros,' Harvey said. 'My dad says there's more homeless now than he's ever seen.'

'No sleeping bags, though,' Ebony said, her camping experience rendering her an authority. 'They've gone, now.'

'Summer's nearly here,' Harvey said. 'Maybe they moved further along the coast? That's what I'd do if I had nowhere to go – sleep on the beach.'

They looked around a little longer but found nothing of interest. When they went back outside, Xavier and Willow were waiting for them.

'Find anything?' Xavier asked.

'Camp beds and mugs,' Ebony said. 'Stuff that shouldn't be here.'

'Same in ours,' Willow said.

'I found the wrapper off a packet of Tim Tams,' Xavier confirmed. 'Pretty sure they didn't have those in olden times.'

'Let's keep looking around,' Ebony said, no longer caring if she was home late. This was the most fun she'd had all year.

They found tyre tracks leading into a stable. They laughed at the names of the pit ponies written on the wall. Badger. Trinket. Lilliput.

'Why would you ride a horse down a mine?' Harvey asked.

'How would you even get it in there?' Xavier said.

'They must've had a lift,' Ebony suggested.

'I think they had a little train with carts for the coal,' Willow said. 'There's a track on that hill over there.'

The kids ran across the paddock to the machinery shed and peered inside. There were ploughs and enormous drills and shelves of rusted hammers and pickaxes. Xavier tried to lift one of the axes, but it was too heavy for him.

'They broke rocks with those, eh?' Harvey said. 'Like convicts.'

'Must've been strong,' Xavier said. 'Wonder if they wore helmets with torches on them?'

The railway track led down the slope and vanished into the dark mouth of the mine. Their stomachs full of butterflies, the four children peered through the slats of the metal gate. The entry was locked with a slide bolt, and a shiny modern padlock was looped through the handle.

'You see anything?' Willow said.

'It's too dark,' Ebony said, switching on the torch on her phone. She shone the device into the gloom. Just inside the entrance, she could make out something stacked against the rock wall, concealed under a blue tarpaulin.

'Could be treasure,' Harvey said excitedly.

'It's someone's stuff,' Xavier said. 'How do we get in for a closer look?'

The children examined the old gate. Harvey crouched and rubbed his palm across the loose dirt.

'Fetch one of those shovels, Xav,' he said. 'If we dig under here, maybe one of us can squeeze through.'

The other three children immediately turned to look at Ebony, who was the smallest.

'I'm not going in there,' Ebony said.

'I dare you,' Harvey said.

'Double dare,' Xavier added.

'There might be poisonous gas or something,' Ebony protested.

'Use your T-shirt as a mask,' Xavier said.

'That won't work against poison,' Willow said, grinning. 'Anyway, don't bother digging. Look at the lock.'

While the other three looked on in amazement, Willow lifted the padlock out of the way and slid the bolt back. The gate yawned open with a menacing creak.

'How did you do that?' Harvey said, astonished and impressed.

'It wasn't locked properly,' Willow said. 'The padlock was on the top loop instead of the bottom one. Dad does it on our side gate all the time.'

Sceptical, Xavier played with the slide bolt mechanism for a moment before smiling as he worked it out.

'Oh, yeah,' he said. 'Someone stuffed up.'

The children stared nervously into the darkness.

'You go first,' Harvey said, nudging Xavier.

'I'm not going first. What if there's a hidden shaft and I fall in?'

'Then you cark it four months early,' Harvey told him.

'Yeah, nah, I don't think so,' Xavier said. 'Eb should go. She has the torch.'

'Get out of the way, then,' Ebony said, raising her phone. Her friends stood aside as she tiptoed tentatively across the threshold. She scanned the stone floor with the torch beam, checking to make sure there were no holes. There was a strong chemical smell in the air, sharp enough to tickle her nostrils. Ebony lifted the edge of the tarpaulin and peered underneath. She found barrels of fertiliser, bottles of clear liquid and two dozen paint tins filled with old nails. Disappointed but curious, she stepped back and cast her torch across the roof of the cavern then down the uneven stone wall, where she noticed a trident symbol crudely carved into the rock. She took photographs of the emblem, as well as snaps of the tarpaulin and what was stored underneath.

'Eb, what do you see?' Harvey hissed.

Ebony turned to the chasm that stretched before her, the tunnel that descended into the hidden depths of the mine. For a moment, she considered farewelling her friends and following the train tracks until her phone battery died. She could find a quiet spot in the darkness and hunker down, waiting for the morning of her ninth birthday to come. Perhaps down there, in the forgotten void, the old gods wouldn't find her, wouldn't make her sing their dying refrain. Perhaps she could escape their clutches and emerge the next day, the sole survivor, blinking against the light.

* * *

EBONY SAT ON HER BED AND CONSIDERED THE FAULT LINES IN the adult world as she saw them, through the jaded eyes of an eight-year-old to whom no one would listen. Her mum Hayley was so full of anger and frustration at being unable to control events, she couldn't hear a word Ebony said. She didn't care how her daughter felt and didn't consider what she might want. Hayley believed in hierarchy, and placed herself firmly at the top. To Ebony, who had yet to be introduced to such terms, her mum was simply bossy and mean. Then there was her other mum, Jude. She had become increasingly distant and melancholic, resigned to inevitability. She would sit next to Ebony on the couch and stroke her hair while weeping. That made Ebony uncomfortable. There would be plenty of time for tears after she was gone. She didn't appreciate being treated like a terminal cancer patient. There was nothing wrong with her. Jude was miserable, and Ebony didn't like knowing she was the cause.

One angry, one sad, neither of them listening. As she whiled away the lonely hours, Ebony felt increasingly relieved that she wouldn't have to endure being part of the adult world. Adults made everything so complicated. They made everything about them.

Ebony lay on her bed staring at the pattern of stars Sky had helped her stick to the ceiling, and vowed to remember that feeling if she somehow managed to live. That feeling of being ignored, underestimated, her opinion being dismissed as unimportant. She had big thoughts, too. Big dreams. Huge hopes. Sparkling ideas. And yet she was treated like an expensive doll with nothing to say, too precious to take out of the box, cute to look at but not worth listening to.

I promise I won't be like them when I grow up, she vowed. *I will be different. I will not forget how this feels.*

There were three short knocks at the door, then the sound of a key turning in the lock. Hayley's face appeared. Ebony glared at her.

'Good news,' she said, sighing. 'Your mum wore me down. She said that given how short your time is, I'm being unreasonable keeping you in here. Even though you were wilfully disobedient in meeting those Peppr brats after I explicitly told you to stay away from them.'

'Hayles . . .' Jude warned from the lounge room.

'Sorry,' Hayley said calmly. She smiled, though it was becoming increasingly difficult for her to do so. 'As you know, Sky is having her eighteenth birthday party this afternoon.'

'Are we going?' Ebony asked eagerly.

'Yes!' Jude shouted from the lounge.

Ebony flopped back on the doona, punching the air in elation.

'Get ready, then,' Hayley said. 'We're leaving in twenty minutes.'

Ebony was so excited she could hardly breathe. She strained to see the ceiling stars in the daylight, remembering the night she and Sky had lain on the bed with the lights out and her half-sister had explained why the stickers were arranged in the shape of a centaur drawing a bow. Ebony was a child of Sagittarius. She had snuggled up to Sky while her half-sister had told her about the nebulae of stars in the constellation. The Lagoon Nebula, the Trifid Nebula, the Red Spider Nebula, the Omega Nebula. Faraway places no human would ever visit.

* * *

IF EBONY WAS OUT OF PLACE AMIDST THE SEVENTEEN- AND eighteen-year-olds at Sky's birthday party, she showed no signs of feeling it. She laughed at their jokes and listened avidly to their conversations, hanging on her half-sister's every word. Hayley eyed her daughter watchfully from her poolside lounger, cocktail hardly touched.

'Quit staring at her,' Jude said. Her margarita glass was already half empty.

'Sorry,' Hayley said, snapping out of her fugue. 'How can she be so comfortable around them?'

'Rude bunch, aren't they?' Dirk said, pulling up a plastic chair. 'Ungrateful, disinterested and dismissive. No idea how fortunate they are.'

'We were like that at their age,' Jude said.

'You were,' Dirk said, grinning. 'I was working in the shop for a pittance, nursing my bruises and about to become a father.'

'I'm sure Sky and her friends love hearing you talk about how tough you had it back in the day,' Jude said.

'I hardly talk to them at all,' Dirk admitted. 'They're so sensitive. One harsh word and they jump on social media complaining about how you're holding them back from becoming a TikTok dance sensation about to secure sponsorship from an energy drink company.'

'Sky doesn't seem too bad,' Hayley said, finally taking a sip of her cocktail.

'Her mum treats her like she's the cool kid at school and she's desperate to be friends with her,' Dirk said, snorting. 'Sky's smart, though. She keeps Luce at arm's length unless she wants something and then grants her brief, exclusive access until her demands have been fulfilled. Then Luce gets plunged back into the fortress of solitude, alongside the other ghosted mums who can't work out what they've done wrong and why their daughter won't talk to them.'

'Don't act like you're immune to her charms,' Jude said. 'If she stabbed someone in the chest seventeen times, you'd stand up in court and claim the victim threw themselves onto the knife.'

Dirk nodded rueful agreement.

'It's true, I'm a sucker,' he said. 'You should see her wardrobe. Full of investment pieces, as she calls them. I might have to sell her shoe collection soon.'

'Business still bad?' Hayley asked.

'Sign of the times, unfortunately,' Dirk said. 'We need a radical rethink of how we approach everything.'

Hayley sipped her drink silently. She did not disagree. She just wished her daughter would be included in the new world order. Dirk was the only person in Ebony's life more confident than Hayley that the girl's inexorable fate could be avoided.

'What do you get an eighteen-year-old who has everything?' Jude asked.

'I'll show you,' Dirk said, beckoning for Sky to come over. His daughter excused herself from her friends and joined them.

'Your dad wants to boast about his gift,' Jude said.

'Oh, this?' Sky said, displaying the watch on her wrist.

Jude whistled.

'That's a twelve-thousand-dollar Santos de Cartier,' Dirk said proudly.

'Isn't it beautiful?' Sky said, holding the watch up to the light.

'Make sure you keep the paperwork,' Dirk told her. 'It'll increase the value if you ever need to sell it.'

'Sell my eighteenth birthday gift from my dad?' Sky said. 'I don't think so. This is coming with me to the grave.'

Dirk put his arm around his daughter's hips and pulled her close.

'I would've bought you a car, but end of the world, and all that,' he said. 'Anyway, once we hit the reset button, we'll be flying around in hydrogen-powered gyrocopters. The combustion engine will be obsolete, more's the pity.'

'It won't be the only thing that's obsolete, if you have your way,' Sky said.

'Bloody oath,' Dirk said. 'This country needs shaking up. In every disaster, there lies opportunity.'

Sky extricated herself from her father's grasp and addressed the group.

'Dad views himself as an integral part of the new regime,' she said, rolling her eyes. 'Most likely its leader.'

'Is there room for us in this utopia?' Jude asked.

'There's room for everyone,' Dirk said, grinning. 'Providing you understand and accept the power structure.'

Jude sighed and slipped her hand into Hayley's.

'Why do I get the sinking feeling that, once again, women will be consigned to the breeding cave while the patriarchs have all the fun?'

'Exactly,' Sky said, plucking a tomato and pesto canapé from a passing plate. Her father had hired an enterprising group of local nonnas as caterers and instructed them to keep salt content to a minimum. They hadn't really listened.

'Not a bit of it,' Dirk said. 'You can fight, Jude. We'll put you in charge of defending the community.'

'You planning on building a wall around Gattan?' Jude said, laughing.

'Hopefully it won't come to that,' Dirk said.

'Defend us from whom?' Hayley asked.

'Those trying to halt progress,' Dirk said. 'You've seen the news. It's madness out there. Terror attacks almost every day, committed by insane people whose only goal is chaos. As if we don't have enough to contend with.'

Dirk pointed to Sky's friends, who were frolicking in the pool or playing on their phones by the buffet.

'Look at these kids,' Dirk said. 'They're the final generation. Alex too. Where is he, anyway?'

'In his room, playing the new *Assassin's Creed*,' Sky said wryly.

'See what I mean?' Dirk said. 'All they know about survival was learnt online or on reality TV. They've never foraged for food, hunted and dressed game, built a shelter or treated infection in the field. They don't even know how to start a fire.'

'Oh, I can light a fire,' Sky said. 'Believe me, I've lit a few.'

'You're saying they require leadership,' Jude said.

'Correct. And structure.'

'With you in charge,' Hayley added.

'Us. With us in charge. The survivors.'

Hayley looked mournfully at her daughter, who was giggling next to a teenage boy twelve years her senior. Dirk caught her gaze.

'I'll deal with that,' he said. 'Don't worry. We'll find a way. I have a few ideas how to protect her.'

'I wish I had your confidence,' Jude said, finishing her drink.

As all eyes fell upon Ebony. Sky chewed her lip, left the adults to mope and decided to check on her sister. She pulled Ebony aside, and they walked to the bottom of the garden and sat on the grass.

'How's things?' Sky asked.

'I'm so happy to be here,' Ebony said. 'Happy birthday. Sorry I didn't get you anything. I've been grounded for days.'

'How come?'

Ebony glanced back at her parents. Hayley was staring at her again.

'You heard of the Peppr app?' she asked.

'Sure,' Sky said, arching an eyebrow. 'They know you're on there?'

'Mum wasn't happy when she found out,' Ebony admitted. 'Mum Jude let me go out to meet my Peppr pals, though.'

'That must have been fun,' Sky said.

'It was,' Ebony said, brightening. 'We were a bit naughty. We went to the mine.'

'The abandoned mine?' Sky said. 'Yeah, I've been there. Pretty cool. Hope none of your friends fell in a hole.'

Ebony glanced at her parents again, then leant in close to Sky.

'I think something's going on out there,' she said.

'How do you mean?'

Ebony took out her phone and showed Sky the photos she had taken. Sky swiped through them idly, then stopped on the one Ebony took inside the cavern. A crease formed on her brow.

'What's this?' she asked.

'I uploaded that one to a Peppr chat,' Ebony said. 'Here, I'll show you. Do you know what it means, what they're saying?'

Sky scrolled through the comments, and the hairs on the back of her neck rose.

'Kingdom of Hades,' she muttered.

'Are they bad people?' Ebony asked.

'Depends on your point of view. Did you show this to your mums?'

Ebony puffed out her cheeks. 'No way,' she said. 'If Mum Hayley knew I went into the mine, I wouldn't even make it to my ninth birthday. She'd kill me on the spot.'

'What about Jude?' Sky asked.

'My mums aren't very good at hearing me right now,' Ebony said sheepishly.

'Hmm,' Sky said. 'That's adults for you. I'm AirDropping this to my phone, Eb. Leave it with me. It's probably nothing, so don't worry, but I'll ask around and see what I can find out.'

'Thank you for listening, Sky,' Ebony said, hugging the older girl.

Sky kissed the top of her head.

'You can always talk to me, little sister,' she said. 'Hey, listen, are you coming to the graduation ball next Saturday?'

'I don't know if I'm allowed,' Ebony said morosely.

'I'll speak to your mums,' Sky said. 'You and all your Peppr pals are invited. We'll have a table of saltless snacks and everything. Dad's turned it into a big community event. The entire town will be there.'

Ebony leapt to her feet with excitement.

'You deserve a party, too,' Sky said.

'It can be for my ninth birthday, only early!' Ebony said.

Despite the warmth of the day, Sky felt a chill course through her blood.

'Absolutely,' she said. 'Now, did you bring your togs?'

Ebony nodded furiously. Sky stood up and took her half-sister by the hand.

'Let's go and get changed,' she said.

Hayley watched as Sky led her daughter into the Van der Saar mansion. Beside her, Dirk and Jude were engaged in an animated discussion about the definition of roles in a post-Orphean society, but she didn't hear a word. She stared instead at the teenage boys skulking by the water's edge, dressed in baggy pants, oversized sneakers, basketball shirts, wraparound sunglasses and baseball caps with stickers still attached to the visor. These reprobates were the future of the planet. The final generation. These bugs on a windshield had no idea what they were up against.

An incessant tapping on her thigh wrested Hayley's attention back to the moment. She blinked as Jude's frowning face came into view. Her lips were moving, but there was no sound other than a persistent buzz.

PART NINE

DON'T LOOK BACK

AS LOCAL COUNCILS ACROSS THE NATION FAILED TO RESPOND to the ongoing crisis in any meaningful way, public meetings became problematic. Following outbreaks of violence, including assault, vandalism and in some cases murder, many cities and towns suspended public assembly. Council matters were discussed privately, behind locked doors and in the presence of security personnel. But that did not stop protesters from demanding action. Angry crowds swarmed local representatives as they left the building, or set their vehicles ablaze. Fearing for the safety of their families, swathes of councillors and mayors resigned, leaving a power vacuum on a local level that led to a breakdown in the delivery of essential services. Garbage was left uncollected on nature strips. Public facilities such as leisure centres closed or fell into disrepair. The grass grew long and wild on untended sporting ovals. No one paid parking fines anymore, and soon they were no longer issued. The potholes in roads grew ever larger, rendering some highways dangerously unnavigable.

The role of councils was supplanted by assemblies of concerned citizens, for the most part Decadians and others personally unaffected by the daily death toll. One such transformation was underway in the town of Gattan. Private meetings were held in town hall chambers to discuss the future direction of the community. These gatherings were by invitation only, organised through a private WhatsApp group. They were attended by prominent local business owners like Dirk van der Saar, who seized the opportunity to reinvent himself as one of the main architects of whatever form society might take moving forward. For that was what he and his fellow upstanding citizens desired – to acknowledge the regrettable situation and establish a plan of action that would guarantee a future for their families and their business interests. They wished to preserve some semblance of the civilisation they had always known, while steering progress to their advantage.

Dirk and his son Alex sat in the back row of the meeting room, waiting for the last of the cabal to arrive. Alex didn't want to be there. He'd rather have been at home playing *Star Wars Outlaws*, but his father insisted he attend. Alex kept his head down, trying to appear as inconspicuous as possible, though he noted the presence of several teenagers in the chamber. He met the gaze of a boy two rows in front who turned to see who was coming through the huge oak door. They smiled awkwardly at each other.

Dirk waited patiently for the convenor to welcome everyone to the meeting and run through the orders of business. Dirk knew the man well. He had played football with him in high school. Gary Oswald owned Tyrepower Gattan and a Total Tools franchise. His businesses were failing, just like Dirk's was. Dirk waited for Gary to call him to the podium as the first speaker for the evening, then winked at Alex as he rose to a smattering of applause and walked to the front of the room.

'Friends, you all know me,' Dirk began. 'Some of your wives knew me too, back in the day.'

This was met with a peal of laughter. Several of the men – the audience was mostly male, and skewed older – shook their heads.

'No, I'm kidding,' Dirk said. 'I've been happily married for almost twenty years, and my family and I have been an integral part of life in Gattan for more than a hundred years. The Van der Saar roots run deep in this town, and I have personally dedicated myself to ensuring Gattan is a thriving, friendly, family-oriented municipality that we're all proud to live in.'

There was a brief round of applause and murmurs of agreement from the assembled citizens.

'We now stand at a crossroads,' Dirk continued. 'A terrible curse has beset our great nation, along with the rest of the world.

The unthinkable has happened. I don't wish to dwell on Orpheus Nine too much because, frankly, that's not what this meeting is about, but obviously our hearts go out to the afflicted and their families. We are truly sorry for their losses, and they are ever present in our thoughts and prayers. My son Alex is here tonight. Put your hand up, mate.'

Surprised by the sudden attention, Alex meekly raised his hand.

'Good lad,' Dirk said. 'Alex is ten years old. He missed the cull by a hair's breadth, and for that, I am thankful and humbled. He'll hate me for saying this, and, believe me, it's not an easy thing for me to reconcile, but he reminds me of my old man. Some of you knew Willem van der Saar. He and I didn't always see eye to eye, but when it came to accepting my familial responsibilities, I stepped up. One day Alex, or my daughter Sky, who just turned eighteen and is about as clever as they come, will take over from me. They are Van der Saars. That's their destiny.

'Now, the reason I say Alex reminds me of Willem is that my old man was obsessed with science fiction. *Star Trek*, *Stargate*, anything with "star" in the title. He'd record shows and stay up late to watch them. I never understood his fascination. But now I see Alex playing games and reading books about other worlds and I wonder if maybe they weren't onto something. Who knows what's happening to our planet right now? Not governments, not scientists and not doctors. My father would've had his theories, of course. And so recently I asked Alex if there was any precedent in science fiction. In his research, he found an Arthur C. Clarke book, *Childhood's End*, in which mankind leaves Earth to start afresh on the far side of the galaxy. It's appropriate for what I want to talk about tonight, friends. Like it or not, the world that we grew up in is gone, and it's not coming back.'

Dirk paused to let his words sink in. The occupants of the council chamber regarded him gravely.

'Supply chains are broken,' Dirk went on. 'There are certain goods that we may never see again in Australia, or at least not for many years to come. The education system has fallen apart. No one sends their kids to school anymore, they're learning everything online. Our hospitals are overrun. There aren't enough medical staff, and that won't be remedied anytime soon. People are dying needlessly while waiting to be seen by a doctor. Infrastructure is failing. How many power outages have we had in the last nine months? More than the previous five years combined. The roads are undriveable. Mobile phone reception is patchy and unreliable. And on top of all this, there are elements within our society who are dedicated to burning everything to the ground. Kingdom of Hades attacks are increasing in frequency. While their anger may be understandable – to a degree – chaos and destruction are not the answer. We need to establish a new order, a system of governance built on integrity, calm and common sense.'

This drew a rousing response from the audience, who clapped and cheered. Dirk accepted the praise before raising his hands for calm.

'I therefore propose the establishment of an independent committee of respected local citizens who will steer Gattan towards a brighter, more hopeful future. It won't be easy, but we need to seriously consider the maintenance of law and control in this town, otherwise everything we've spent our lives working towards will amount to nothing. For the sake of our children, we cannot afford to let what we've built come crumbling down. We need to stand up, be strong, and show the people in this community we love so dearly that we can and will take care of business. Gattan will endure. We may be isolated, but we can be a self-sufficient, prosperous town, free from outside interference. In that regard, I believe we also need to consider founding a local militia. I understand that seems extreme, but I'd like you to think about how we might protect the interests of the community in the absence of traditional officers of the law. We know neither the state nor federal government is going to lift a finger to help rural communities like Gattan. They're all talk and, in any case, are in complete turmoil. We can't rely on them. We're on our own.'

The nodding heads in the audience told Dirk that his speech had hit the mark.

'In brighter news, we're having a graduation ball in this very building on Saturday,' he said. 'Our high school graduates face an uncertain future, so I think it's appropriate that we celebrate their achievements. They will be leaders in the final generation, so we must nurture their talents and, as elders, provide whatever guidance we can. I see this party as a chance for unity within our district. We've invited parents and children of all ages, and I urge you to come along and show your faces, so the transition process may begin.

'That's about it from me, friends. Thanks for allowing me to speak, and for being such receptive listeners. We can do this together. Back to you, Gary.'

Everyone in the chamber rose to their feet and applauded as Dirk returned to his seat.

'Great speech, Dad,' Alex said, impressed.

'Don't tell anyone, but Sky helped me write it,' he whispered, putting an arm around his son's shoulders.

None of the remaining guests spoke as forcefully as Dirk. At the end of the meeting, he was surrounded by wellwishers. The talk was of casting a vote to elect Dirk as leader of the nascent New Gattan Assembly. It was almost dark by the time Dirk and Alex stepped out onto the pavement, but it was a warm, pleasant evening. The horizon glowed red as father and son set off on foot along Watt Street, towards home.

'You were really great, Dad,' Alex said, buoyed by the attention.

'Thanks, mate,' Dirk said. 'Bit out of my comfort zone, to be honest, but I don't think we're going to have much choice in the matter. The way things are going, I'll probably have to shutter the business. No one's buying earrings when the world's ending.'

'Is it ending?'

'These past few years, there's always been something,' Dirk said. 'Orpheus Nine is just the latest in a long string of disasters that grab everyone's attention. The trick is to focus on what matters for you and not get caught up in everyone else's shit. We're at the start of something new. We just don't know exactly what that will look like yet.'

'Are you going to be in charge?' Alex asked.

'Someone has to be,' Dirk replied. 'Might as well be me. I was captain of the footy team, you know.'

'What will happen to Ebony?' Alex asked hesitantly.

'We're going caving after the graduation ball,' Dirk told him.

'Caving?'

'Yeah, there's a cave system in the hills about three hours east of here,' Dirk told him. 'You, me, Jude, Hayley and Ebony will camp there for a few nights. We'll go deep below the earth to protect Eb from the wave when it sweeps through. It'll be hard, but other people have done it. So I'm told, anyway.'

'Do we go down on ropes?' Alex asked.

'Absolutely. I've hired all the gear, and we've even got a professional cave diver to take us in. It'll be an adventure.'

'Cool,' Alex said, although he found the prospect of rappelling into a subterranean cave system terrifying.

'You're not scared, are you?' Dirk asked.

'A bit, but I'll still go,' Alex said. 'I don't want Ebony to die.'

'She won't,' Dirk assured him. 'That girl has Van der Saar blood. We're survivors.' Dirk glanced down at his son as they walked through the housing estate towards Jongebloed Lane. 'When we're there, I'd like to see some leadership from you, Alex.'

'What do you mean?'

'Like, maybe you volunteer to go first into a cave? Show everyone what you're made of. Set a good example for Ebony.'

'I guess,' Alex said, unconvinced.

'You heard what I said in the meeting about forming a militia, right? You know what that is?'

Alex nodded. 'They talk about militias in a game called *Rainbow Six*.'

'Right, well, it's going to be like that, only in real life,' Dirk told him.

'Will they have guns?'

'Probably not at first, but eventually, it might be necessary,' Dirk said, musing aloud to himself. 'We'll have to work out how to get those. Damon Braithwaite's son is in the army. Maybe he can hook us up.'

'Aren't guns illegal, Dad? It's not like America.'

'We'll be making the rules from now on, Alex,' Dirk told him. 'You're pretty good with weapons, eh? Better shot than me.'

'That's just in games, though,' Alex said. 'I've never fired a gun for real. Never even seen one.'

'That'll change when you're in the militia,' his father said. Alex gawped, eyes wide as they turned the corner into Jongebloed Lane. 'All those online shooters will hold you in good stead, Alex. We'll organise training camps, of course. Teach you survival skills. It'll be like the Boy Scouts, only hardcore. It's already happening in other towns. We need to stand up for ourselves in Gattan. Not everyone's going to embrace what's coming, Alex, but there's no denying the facts. You're the last generation, son. You will have to stand ready.'

'Ready for what?' Alex asked, but he already knew the answer. He had played enough games and read enough books to recognise that a war was brewing, and that by virtue of his birthdate, one week before his friends who had died in the first wave, his side had already been chosen.

* * *

ON THE NIGHT OF THE GRADUATION BALL, THE TOWN HALL WAS packed. Approximately one hundred children were present, accompanied by their parents. Everyone had dressed in their finery for the grand occasion, although the stars of the show were undoubtedly the graduating eighteen-year-olds and the dozen eight-year-olds in attendance. Both of those groups were thrilled to be the centre of attention, for different reasons. Ebony had bathed in body glitter. Her mass of curls was contorted into a 1980s Whitney Houston tribute hairstyle. She was so amped, she hyperventilated in the car on the way and had to stand outside the hall with her mothers to catch her breath before entering the fray. Her Peppr pals Xavier, Harvey and Willow were also present. They congregated next to a table of saltless snacks manned by Lucy van der Saar, in sorrowful solidarity with the little ones who only had weeks to live.

Sky van der Saar and her friends stayed close to the stage, keeping their distance from the uncool adults. Sky's light pulsed brightest amongst the group. She wore a black Prada dress and white Maison Margiela Tabi flats, accessorised with her Cartier watch and a set of Lucy's pearls. Hayley, Jude and Dirk observed the teenagers from afar, each sipping a glass of Prosecco.

'We were never that glamorous,' Jude said.

'She looks like a million bucks,' Hayley agreed.

'More like twenty grand, in that outfit,' Dirk muttered. 'You wouldn't believe the hoops I had to jump through to find the designer gear she wanted. You can't get that stuff anymore. It's ridiculous. We're not attending the Met Gala.'

'Let them have their night,' Jude said.

A photographer from *The Sentinel* herded the graduates under a banner that read: CONGRATULATIONS, CLASS OF '23.

'Oh, look,' Hayley said sarcastically. 'Your daughter will finally appear in next week's "Out and About in Gattan" section. Life goal achieved.'

'Yeah, we'll be the talk of the RSL,' Dirk said. He regarded Jude and Hayley mischievously. 'I was going to suggest that the banner should say "Class of O9" instead, but I thought maybe that was a bit on the nose.'

'Don't make jokes about it, Dirk,' Hayley snapped.

'Easy, babe,' Jude said.

Hayley was struggling to focus on the event. She was itching to pack up the car and head off on their caving trip. Dirk had almost convinced her the strategy would work. She was ninety per cent certain that by isolating her daughter deep underground, the invisible wave of death would pass harmlessly overhead. If Ebony lived, she had promised herself she would work tirelessly to provide her child with everything she ever wanted or needed. Hayley would be the best mother in the world. That was all she yearned for. But she couldn't allow herself to imagine that version of herself yet. That woman was a stranger Hayley had yet to meet, and if the trip went south, if her daughter started singing in the depths of darkness, then Hayley thought she might stay down there herself. Unhook her carabiner from the rope and cast herself into the abyss.

Jude watched Ebony chatting to Lucy van der Saar at the saltless table. Her daughter was polite and gracious, humming with palpable excitement. Jude caught Lucy glancing enviously at her own girl, over by the stage, throwing her head back in laughter. Even though Jude believed there was a chance Ebony might survive – a slim one, maybe ten per cent – for months, she had been steeling herself for the agonising rupture every parent in her position faced. She would likely not witness her daughter maturing into a young woman. She would not experience that longing etched in Lucy's desperate expression, of wanting to be friends with her adult offspring while being quietly, devastatingly spurned. Jude wondered if it was a blessing in disguise that she would miss out on that painful rejection. In her dreams, Ebony would only ever be her perfect little girl, unaltered by the onset of pubescent hormones. She would be frozen in time, like a ship in a bottle.

'I told you, don't worry,' Dirk said. 'We'll head off on Monday and everything will be okay, you'll see.'

'What about those other kids?' Hayley said, watching Ebony and her Peppr pals bopping their heads in time to the music.

'We can't save everyone,' he told her.

Dirk didn't much want to, either. He was only interested in saving one child, the girl his old schoolfriend and her partner had conceived with his help. Ebony wasn't his daughter, not really, not in the way Sky was his flesh and blood, but she still carried his genetic material, and that was reason enough to preserve her life. Dirk believed that in the years to come, people would stop having children. There would be no point. Sky and Alex would be the last of their kind. If he could add additional Van der Saar DNA to that list, all the better. He caught Sky's eye from across the room and raised his glass. His daughter smiled and did the same, standing apart from her friends. *Look at them*, Dirk thought, *huddling together for safety like emperor penguins sheltering from a blizzard*. Sky was the best of them. They'd had their fair share of arguments as she navigated her teenage years, but that was no different from any father and daughter. Sky was strident, forceful, adamant in her beliefs, wry and intelligent. He admired her so much. Loved her, really, more than anything. More than Lucy or Alex. That boy required moulding. He was a long way from where Dirk needed him to be.

'Alex, why don't you go and mingle?' he suggested.

His son, who had been skulking around his father's heels all evening, did not do well in social situations, especially since watching his friends die on the football oval back in March. The expensive therapist had told Dirk the boy needed time to overcome such extreme trauma, but nine months had passed, and he still spent all his waking hours in his room, blowing off virtual limbs.

'And take that tie off,' Dirk told him. 'You look like a Jehovah's Witness.'

Lucy had dressed Alex in formal wear that made her son squirm with discomfort. Relieved, he removed the black tie and handed it to his father, who folded it up and put it in the pocket of his blazer.

'Scoot,' Dirk shooed him away. 'Go make some real friends.'

Alex pushed through the tangle of people to seek out boys his own age. Dirk peered imperiously across the crowd, satisfied that his plans were coming to fruition. None of this would have happened without his intervention, persistence and guidance. He was the man of the hour. A pillar of the community. He would probably win citizen of the year. And if he saved Ebony, he would be a hero. Someone worth electing as leader, a man capable of ushering in a bold new age. He checked the time on his Rolex Datejust and downed the dregs of his Prosecco. It was almost time for his speech.

* * *

THE CAR PARK WAS FULL WHEN JESS AND GEORGIA ARRIVED. JESS waited by the entrance, the van's engine idling, while Georgia circled the parking lot in her Falcon, looking for a space. Inside, the party was in full swing. Bursts of music blasted from within whenever someone opened the door to step outside for a smoke. Jess had painted a crude approximation of the catering company's logo on the side of the van, and no one paid the late arrivals the slightest attention. Georgia pulled up next to the van and wound down the window.

'Nowhere to park,' she said, chewing a nail nervously. 'We should have come earlier.'

'Try across the road, next to the park,' Jess suggested.

'Won't be very effective over there,' Georgia said.

'We'll catch them when they're running out,' Jess said. 'It'll be bedlam. Go on, I'll wait for you.'

Georgia nodded and drove out of the car park. She performed a loop of the street and came back, eventually finding a spot halfway up the hill outside the entrance to the council offices. She cut the engine and hopped out, pausing to wince at how low the rear end of the vehicle was sitting. Locking the door, she then jogged down the hill towards the van.

'Just walk,' Jess muttered. She didn't want to attract attention.

Georgia opened the passenger door and hauled herself into the cab. Her hands were shaking.

'Calm down,' Jess told her.

'Easier said than done.'

Jess put the van into gear and trundled through the car park until they came to the loading dock.

'Jump down and unhook that chain,' she told Georgia.

'There's probably cameras here,' Georgia said, glancing up at the lights on the side of the building.

'Doesn't matter,' Jess said. 'They'll know who's responsible. Make sure you look up and smile.'

'I want my good side on the news,' Georgia joked. She stepped down and dragged the chain across so Jess could pull in behind the other catering vans. Jess switched off the engine and sat back in the seat, taking several deep breaths as Georgia got back into the van. They sat in silence for a moment, trying not to think about the fact that there were enough explosives behind them to level half the street.

'We don't have to do this,' Georgia said.

'I know.'

'We could drive away now, no harm done.'

'I know.'

'A lot of people are going to die,' Georgia said.

'I said *I know*,' Jess told her.

'Are you sure we're doing the right thing here, mate?'

Jess shook her head. 'I can't tell anymore. I don't know who I am. The person I used to be is gone. Died on that footy field, next to her son. I'm just trying to move forward.'

Georgia clenched her teeth and exhaled.

'Yeah, me too,' she said. 'Listen, I've been thinking. We don't need to be here when it happens. We can detonate remotely. If we sacrifice ourselves, the movement loses our experience. You're one of the best trainers we have, Jess. Hades needs women like you. It seems a waste.'

Jess turned to face her comrade.

'You're right, it is a shame, but every day thousands of new Orpheans come into being. There will be more and more like me, enough to form a tidal wave that will wipe everything clean. Can't you see that if we don't do this, they'll never listen? They'll just wait until every child is dead, and then who are we? Nobodies. The forgotten people, shells, consigned to our sad little lives while they prosper. They don't care about us, so I don't care about them.' Tears streamed down Jess's cheeks. 'I can't take it anymore, Georgia. I want to die. I want them to see me, really see me. I want them to know what it's like to suffer.'

Racked with sobs, Georgia reached across to embrace her friend. They pressed their foreheads together and dried each other's tears.

'Don't look back,' Georgia said, sniffling.

'Don't look back,' Jess replied.

They let go of each other and climbed out of the van. Jess opened the rear doors. Inside were six barrels of ammonium nitrate mixed with wood pulp, saltpetre and ethylene glycol dinitrate. Jess took out her phone and opened the PDF containing the instructions. They had secured a burner phone to one of the barrels along with a simple detonator that would be triggered by the vibration of the ringing handset. Jess followed the directions to activate the detonator. The LED on the dial switched from red to green.

'That's it, I think,' she said.

'Both phones charged?' Georgia asked.

Jess checked her phone. Seventy-three per cent battery life. She closed the rear doors and locked the van, then threw the keys into the darkness.

'One final smoke?' Georgia suggested, holding up a packet of Winfield Blues.

'Those things will kill you,' Jess said.

The two women walked up the ramp and reattached the chain before wandering through the car park to the nature strip beyond. Georgia handed Jess a cigarette and lit it for her, then took one herself. They inhaled deeply. Jess coughed and looked up at the night sky. There were no clouds, just a panoply of stars. She remembered those lazy nights in the dunes overlooking Windmill Creek and Outlook Beach, back when she had friends who loved her. The wind blowing in off the surf, carrying the briny smell of the ocean. Goosebumps rising on her skin as she lay on the damp sand, curling a million grains between her fingers and toes. The lips of a lover on her neck. The laughter of a best mate. The bracing pleasure of running into the sea and being enveloped by the roaring silence. She had everything to live for. So much promise. It had all led to this moment. Now, she was about to have her very own Thanos moment. A click of the fingers. A flash of light, and everything crumbles.

* * *

THE APPLAUSE SUBSIDED AS DIRK LEANT INTO THE MICROPHONE. His first word caused a squeal of feedback that made everyone wince. He removed the device from its stand and curled the cord around his wrist, holding the mic away from his mouth.

'Can everyone hear me okay?' he asked.

'As long as you're not going to sing,' someone shouted, to a ripple of laughter.

'I'm not good at everything,' Dirk said, eliciting audible groans. Sky rolled her eyes from the front row. 'Look, I'll keep this brief.

I just wanted to extend my gratitude to all of you for coming tonight. It means a lot to see our community so united in the face of adversity. It's easy to get caught up in pessimism preached by doomsayers, so being able to organise a positive event that's inclusive of everyone is, I think, essential for our mental health and wellbeing. God knows this town has endured some tough times of late, and the struggle is ongoing. But it's heartening to see a new generation of fresh young faces who will help steer us through the challenges towns like Gattan are going to encounter. Many of them are here tonight, young innovators graduating from high school during the most turbulent year we've ever known – even worse than Covid! Remember when that was all we were worried about?'

Dirk paused for the crowd to laugh and shake their heads. *I'm getting good at this speech lark*, he thought. *Missed my true calling.*

'On a personal note, my beautiful daughter Sky is here. Hopefully I won't get teary and embarrass her, but your mother and I love you, Sky. You've turned out to be an amazing young woman. I'm so fucking proud of you, and I can't wait to see what you achieve. We're here for you, no matter what. You, and all your friends here tonight, are the future. And we have no doubt you'll make us proud. Thank you, everyone, and have a great night.'

Dirk clambered down from the stage to warm applause. Sky unabashedly hugged her father.

'I love you too, Dad,' she said. 'Even though you're a manipulative prick.'

Dirk's heart practically burst.

'Like father, like daughter,' he told her, grinning so widely his ears popped.

'Nice speech, but I'd make a few edits,' she said. 'If you need a campaign manager, I'm available.'

'Honestly, that's the best idea I've heard in ages,' Dirk said. 'You're hired.'

'I have certain salary expectations, commensurate with my ability to make you sound like a benevolent dictator instead of a small-town ignoramus.'

'Even more hired,' Dirk said. 'You're eighteen now, mate. I think it's time you and I sat down to discuss the family trust.'

'I'll speak to my legal team,' Sky said, smiling. 'Hey, listen, Dad, can I come with you on the caving trip? I want to be there for Ebony, just in case the worst happens.'

'Think you can handle it?' Dirk asked, impressed by her request.

'I was next to you at the footy ground when it started,' she said. 'I want to see it through, especially for her. She's one of us.'

Dirk pulled his daughter into his chest.

'Good girl,' he said. 'Of course you can come. Thank you. It'll mean a lot to Ebony and her mums.'

'Speaking of which, where is my little sister?' Sky said, looking around.

She detached herself from her father and squeezed through the heaving mass of bodies to the saltless table, where Ebony and her Peppr pals were having the time of their young lives. Ebony practically leapt into Sky's arms when she saw her.

'You're having fun, I take it?' Sky said, laughing.

'*So* much fun.' Ebony showed Sky the paper plate full of snacks. 'These are way better than those yucky muesli bars Mum used to make.'

'Oh, I don't know,' Sky said. 'I quite liked the one with cranberry and white chocolate. Shame cranberries became impossible to source. Jeez, it's hot in here, isn't it?'

Sky tugged at her decolletage, acutely aware that her Prada dress was acquiring sweat stains that might never wash out. The garment was supposed to be dry clean only.

'I know, I'm boiling,' Ebony said.

Sky took her hand.

'Come outside for some fresh air,' she said. 'I have something to show you.'

Sky led her half-sister through the crowd to the kitchen. They walked past the catering team of disgruntled nonnas, several of whom frowned disapprovingly at the intrusion.

'Why are we going this way?' Ebony asked.

'Too many stinky smokers out front,' Sky said.

The hubbub dulled to a distant murmur as they came to the side door of the town hall. Sky pushed through the emergency exit, and they came out onto the loading dock. Three white vans were parked in the alley. Sky led Ebony past them towards a dark spot away from the light, beside the recycling bins. She crouched next to the younger girl.

'Look up,' she said.

Ebony cast her eyes to the heavens and gawped at the panorama of flickering lights set against an obsidian sky.

'We don't even know how many stars there are in the galaxy,' Sky said. 'It could be as many as four hundred billion.'

'That's a lot,' Ebony said.

'It is,' Sky agreed. 'Remember when I helped you create the Sagittarius constellation on the ceiling of your bedroom? Look, there it is.'

Sky pointed to the stars, moving Ebony's head so she could look along the length of her arm.

'I see it!' she said excitedly.

'In Ancient Greece, they believed that stars were gods. They watched us from above. And if we listened, we might gain wisdom.'

'Is that what Orpheus Nine is about?' Ebony asked. 'Do the gods want me to join them?'

'Maybe,' Sky said, heartsore at the thought. 'Some people believe that, but no one knows.'

'Will I become a star, Sky?'

'Yes,' Sky said, unable to hold back a tear. Ebony reached up and gathered the droplet on her fingertip. She held it to her lips.

'Salty,' she said. 'Don't cry, Sky. I'm not afraid.'

'You're such a brave girl,' Sky said. 'I wish we had more time.'

Sky buried her face in Ebony's hair. Her intention had been to comfort her half-sister, to help ease her through the difficult days to come. Instead, she was the one being consoled.

'The sign on that van looks funny,' Ebony said.

Sky sniffed back tears and turned to see what Ebony was talking about. The third van, the one parked behind the others, was old and dirty. The logo for Gattan and District Catering was the wrong size and painted askew. Sky stood and smoothed down her dress. She approached the van for a closer look. Shielding her eyes with both palms, Sky peered through the back windows. Inside were six barrels, one with a mobile phone attached. A green light blinked repeatedly.

Sky inhaled sharply and stepped back, grabbing Ebony's hand.

'What is it?' Ebony asked.

'We need to hurry,' Sky said. 'Kingdom of Hades are here.'

* * *

PRECIOUS MINUTES PASSED WHILE SKY FORCED HER WAY through the mass of bodies assembled inside the hall. She held Ebony's hand tightly, practically dragging her through the maze of people dancing to Beyoncé's 'Break My Soul' track, oblivious to the imminent danger. To her immense relief, her father was lingering by the saltless snack table, deep in conversation with Ebony's mothers. Sky took a breath to compose herself before speaking, aware of how insane she might sound.

'There's going to be an attack,' she told the three adults.

Hayley, Jude and Dirk stared uncomprehendingly at her.

'Say again?' Dirk said, leaning towards his daughter to better hear her over the loud music.

'I'm getting my friends,' Ebony said to Sky, slipping out of her grasp. Sky let her go, focused on convincing the adults of the danger. Ebony squirmed away towards her Peppr pals.

Sky moved in closer to the adults.

'Listen to me,' she said. 'There's a van parked in the alley, and it's packed with homemade explosives. I couldn't see very well through the window, but it looks like there's a detonator attached to a mobile phone. I think Kingdom of Hades are going to carry out a terror attack.'

Dirk, Hayley and Jude exchanged glances.

'Here, at a graduation ball in Gattan?' Dirk asked. 'Come on, mate, don't fuck around. It's not funny.'

Jude regarded Sky with suspicion.

'Kingdom of Hades usually target cities,' she said. 'I don't see what they'd gain by carrying out an attack in such a small town. If this is a prank, Sky, your dad's right, it's in poor taste.'

'Are you fucking serious?' Sky said, losing her temper. 'I'm telling you what I just saw. That device could go off any minute. You need to listen to me and quietly evacuate without causing a panic. One of their adepts could be here, and if we spook them, a lot of people will die. This is not a joke. Please listen to me.'

'One of them *is* here,' Hayley said.

Dirk, Jude and Sky turned to see who Hayley was looking at. Jess had entered the building, and was discreetly making her way through the crowd, heading towards the far wall. The van was parked on the other side. She was clutching a mobile phone in her hand.

'There's another one by the door,' Jude said.

A dishevelled woman lurked just inside the entrance, looking nervously around the room.

'That's Georgia Slater,' Hayley said. 'She's an Orphean too.'

'Jesus fucking Christ,' Dirk said. 'We'll never get everyone out of here in time. We have to stop them.'

Dirk was about to plunge into the crowd after Jess when his daughter caught him by the arm.

'Dad, no,' she said. 'We can't risk startling her.'

'Each of us approach from a different angle,' Jude said. 'We jump her all at once. We need that phone.'

Dirk nodded agreement. It was clear from the expression on Hayley's face that if she got her hands on Jess, she would tear her to pieces.

Hayley, Jude, Dirk and Sky slipped between the unaware revellers, trying not to draw attention to themselves as they approached Jess, who had positioned herself against the wall and was staring at the parquetry floor, shoulders rising and falling as she psyched herself up to make the call. Dirk desperately pushed against the partygoers but became entangled in the crowd. Sky got there first.

Standing before her at the edge of the crowd were Ebony and her Peppr pals. Xavier, Harvey, Willow, Ebony and eight other children linked hands and silently formed a semicircle around Jess.

Dirk, Jude and Hayley burst from the mass of heaving bodies. A few people in the crowd were beginning to realise that something was happening.

'Stay back,' Sky told them sternly.

Shaking her head, Jess looked up to meet the gaze of twelve eight-year-old kids. She glanced briefly over their heads and clocked Hayley, Jude and Dirk. Lips trembling, she cocked her head to one side and smiled. Then she ignored the adults and concentrated on the children who had her surrounded.

'You can't stop it,' she said. 'You're all dead anyway.'

Ebony let go of Willow and Harvey's hands and stepped forward until she was standing directly in front of Jess.

'We want to live,' she said, looking up at the shattered woman. 'If only for a while. Please don't steal what little time we have left.'

Ebony opened her arms to Jess, offering a moment of kindness. Jess cracked and crouched to hug the girl, tears streaming down her face.

'I'm sorry, Ebony,' she said. 'But I'm already dead too. This is for the best.'

As Jess fumbled with her phone, Ebony snatched at the device. They wrestled for it and fell, the phone tumbling from Jess's grasp. As Jess scrabbled to retrieve it, Ebony kicked it away, sending it skidding across the floor towards Sky, who bent down and scooped it up in one smooth movement. The rest of the Peppr pals swarmed Jess, pinning her down while she screamed in anguished protest.

Panic surged through the crowd as people rushed for the exit. Georgia was caught up in the sudden exodus. Dirk called for someone to restrain her and confiscate her phone. Half-a-dozen people descended angrily on the woman, punching and jostling until she too was lying stunned on the ground.

Jude ran forward and pulled the children aside, throwing herself onto Jess's back and wrapping an arm around her throat in a chokehold. Hayley retrieved Ebony, holding her daughter close.

'You did so good,' she said.

'Are there any more of you?' Jude hissed in Jess's ear. 'Tell me, or I'll break your fucking neck.'

Struggling for breath, Jess shook her head and laughed.

'You think this is funny?' Dirk said, as the hall began to empty out. 'What were you thinking, Jess?'

'She's crazy,' Hayley said. 'Has been for years.'

Jude relaxed the chokehold and Jess fell face down on the polished wooden floor, gasping. She rolled over onto her back, still laughing as the parents of Ebony's Peppr pals collected their children. Lucy appeared by her husband's side. Everyone glared at the woman lying on the floor, appalled by the unthinkable act she had almost committed, the disaster that had almost befallen their community.

Jess rolled onto all fours and snarled. She fixed her gaze on Dirk and Lucy, her chin flecked with spittle.

'I was pregnant when you two met,' she said.

Lucy turned questioningly to her husband. Dirk's eye twitched, his fury subsiding.

'What are you talking about?' he said.

'Oh, don't worry, I lost the baby,' Jess said. 'But at least I knew I could get pregnant. That's why, years later, when I wanted to have a kid, I dragged you into bed, Dirk. Steve didn't have it in him, but you? Everyone knows you're the most fertile man in Gattan.'

The assembled group looked at each other. Eyes widened as the truth became apparent. Lucy's expression changed to one of disgust.

'Tyler was my son?' Dirk said hesitantly, his mind racing. The son he never knew. The boy he watched die. Grief and shock washed over him. No, he thought, it's not possible. It can't be. The Van der Saars are winners.

Sky was rooted to the spot. She and Ebony had prevented a Kingdom of Hades terror attack. They had saved everyone.

And they had another brother, thanks to their wayward father, that egocentric fool. Sky recalled the look in Tyler's eyes when he froze on the football field that day, the paralysis of that horror.

She reached down and clutched Ebony's hand in hers, squeezing her half-sister's warm fingers. Just then she began to hear it in her head. Felt it take hold and move through her – that doom-laden phrase that had gripped the world.

As flies to wanton boys are we to the gods; They kill us for their sport.

The clock ticked over to 8 pm. Exactly nine months and nine hours after Tyler and all those other nine-year-olds had died in a moment of sublime terror.

The next wave was upon them.

THE CYCLE OF NINE

OVER THE COURSE OF HER EIGHTEEN YEARS, SKY VAN DER SAAR often found herself wondering what happened to people when they aged. At what point did they sever their connection with colour, beauty and sadness? When did the moment come to block out sensation, to push their feelings down so deeply inside the well of themselves that they created a vortex, a kaleidoscopic maelstrom of secrets and whispers that inexorably clawed at the light behind their eyes until their gaze turned lifeless, detached from emotion, bereft of passion?

Sky always promised herself it would not happen to her. She would pause daily to soak in the world, allowing herself to feel all the pain and joy and happiness and despair. These conflicting emotions were part of a whole. Hurt could not exist without bliss. On the morning of her final day, she stopped in the street to watch sunlight reflecting off a shop window in such a manner that she caught a glimpse of another world existing alongside her own. A place populated by beings not dissimilar to humans and yet with a corporeal form entirely different from theirs.

Sky could not see, feel or hear those entities. They had made the same scientific progress as her species, had the same railways, houses, telephones and fast-food outlets, all of which were composed of different matter, unknown to humans. Sometimes, Sky would catch a tiny, almost imperceptible movement out of the corner of her eye, but when she looked closer, it would be gone. This was the secret world of possibility. A place of great wonders, of light and harmony, a place where truth was prized, where no one died from negligence or neglect. When Sky awoke in the mornings, she could sometimes feel the presence of these others watching over her, sad smiles on their pure, clean, celestial faces. And then she would blink and yawn and check her phone and the connection would dissipate, leaving behind a lingering sense that something was missing from her life, something undefinable that she couldn't quite wrap her head around. Something wonderful, tantalisingly out of reach. What remained was a feeling of endless promise, laden with regret.

As the buzzing inside her head increased in volume, Sky closed her eyes to block out the noise, then opened them again, faster than she ever had before, taking everything in at once in a flood of sensation. She could feel the silent hum of machinery. She could feel falcon eggs incubating on the ledge of a building in the city. The eggs were tiny, tea-stained things. Sky had heard that if you held a falcon egg up to your lips and made soft chirping noises, the chick would respond. As her eyes rolled back in her head, she saw the world from the perspective of the brooding mother falcon, guarding the nest while the tiercel hunted. The bird swivelled her head at the sound of a car alarm going off in the street below. Wind ruffled her wings, which she folded across her body as she shifted on the eggs to keep them warm.

Sky imagined herself standing on the grass at the bottom of the garden. She looked up at the night sky and located Jupiter. There, just above Libra, to the right of Antares, between twin stars Zubenelgenubi and Zubeneschamali. Arabic words, signifying the southern and northern claws of the scorpion. Zubeneschamali was the only green star in the heavens. She lay one hundred and sixty light years from Earth, and her luminosity was one hundred and thirty times that of the sun. Born half a millennium too early, Sky knew she would never break free from the bonds of Earth and claim her rightful place amongst the stars.

She felt a fizzle in her blood. A ripple coursing through her body as every muscle seized and she became frozen in place.

So, this is what it feels like, she thought. *How strange.* And it was happening to all her friends too. A vibration in her chest became sound, became song.

Lascivi pueri ad muscas deis sumus
Nos ad ludibrium necant

A tempest brewed in Sky van der Saar's bloodstream. If she could have laughed at the irony, she would have done so. *Yes,* she thought. *Yes. Spare my sister. Take me instead. Let her live. I am ready. I am not afraid.*

She could not hear the screams. She could only witness the bittersweet relief on Hayley's and Jude's faces. The tears on Ebony's cheeks. *Go well, little sister,* she thought, as the wall of crackling blue flame crept closer. *It's up to you now.*

'You see?' Jess bellowed above the din, as parents tore at their static, singing eighteen-year-olds, begging them to stop. 'The cycle of nine is real! It's real!'

Dirk van der Saar stood before his daughter. He gripped her by the shoulders, eyes bloodshot and pooled with emotion.

'No,' he said. 'Please, no.'

Sky wanted to throw her arms around her father's neck and reassure him that everything would be all right, that he was a good dad, despite his myriad faults, that her life had been enough. But she could not. The end was near. She had to go.

I'm coming, Zubeneschamali, Sky thought. *I will become lost in your emerald heart.*

She opened her mouth and sang once more.

Lascivi pueri ad muscas deis sumus
Nos ad ludibrium necant

There was a moment of stillness. Her last. Her favourite. And then, her hands and neck began to swell, and a lightning strike of exquisite pain flashed across every fibre of her being. Her pulse quickened. Sky felt all of it, every echoing voice.

Then the wave crashed over her, and she was gone.

ZUBENESCHAMALI

THE LIGHT WITHIN THE CAVE TURNED GOLDEN AND SLOWLY dimmed with the onset of dusk. Pencil torch in hand, Ebony eagerly awaited the exodus of microbats. Thousands of common bent-wing bats roosted in the cave system, and every night after sunset they roused themselves from torpor, stretched their long, leathery wings and took flight.

'Don't move,' Hayley whispered in her ear. 'Stand really still and let them fly past you.'

'Don't worry, they won't crash into you,' Jude assured her.

'I know that,' Ebony said. 'They navigate by echolocation.'

Jude grinned at Hayley, her face glowing in the firelight. Their campsite was small and discreet, so as not to disturb the delicate ecosystem within the caves. It was one of those warm early summer evenings, but Jude had still lit a fire to ward off the chill within the cave. They would snuggle into their sleeping bags for one more night. Then it would be safe to leave. It already was, but Jude and Hayley wanted to be sure no harm would befall their daughter. Better safe than sorry. Jude thought back to the mass funeral they had attended for the eighteen-year-olds of Gattan. Three hundred thousand had perished in Australia. Ninety-six million worldwide. But the loss of Sky hurt the most. Dirk, Lucy and Alex were devastated. So much promise gone in an instant.

Jess was in the wind. No one had seen her since that night. She was the least of Gattan's problems.

For Jude and Hayley, the previous nine days had been bittersweet. The overwhelming feeling of relief was tempered by the realisation that the world was even more broken than anyone had realised. There was no reasoning behind what was happening, no solution in sight. The cycle of nine was real, that much was certain. In nine months and nine hours' time, the wave looked likely to pass on to claim 27-year-olds, then it would be 36-year-olds, 45-year-olds, and so on, until, finally, the 99-year-olds would succumb, and the voice of Orpheus fell silent. By that stage, more than a billion humans would be dead, and the planet would be a very different place. For better or worse, now hundreds of millions of adults knew how and when they would die.

It was beyond comprehension, and so, leaving their devices at home, Hayley, Jude and Ebony struck out for nature: they fled to the cave system three hours east of Gattan, to reflect upon and try to absorb their new reality. In the car, Ebony had asked her mothers if they would be okay. Jude had done the math. They were safe, unless something changed. Rumours were certainly already circulating online of an O9 variant, a mutation that could affect those outside the cycle of nine.

The world may have been broken, but they had been blessed with a narrow reprieve, and they weren't going to waste the opportunity to give their daughter a rich and full life. Like so many others, they vowed to begin again.

'They're coming,' Ebony said. 'Listen.'

Jude rose and stood by her wife and daughter. She held Hayley's hand, squeezing her fingers. Ebony extinguished her torch as the rustling of leathery bat wings increased in volume. And then, suddenly, they were surrounded by thousands of tiny flying mammals, each bat so small they could nestle in the palm of Ebony's hand. They swarmed past the three humans in a rush of flapping wings. It was like being plunged into a snowstorm, but without flakes settling on them. The bats swept past, treating the family like any other obstacle. The tips of their wings flicked at Ebony's hair and she so badly wanted to squeal in delight but was scared to open her mouth in case a bat flew in.

The bats passed them to swirl upwards in a great tornado towards the mouth of the cave and out into the open air beyond.

Ebony turned and ran after the colony, clambering up the rocky path to the entrance.

'No, Ebony, wait!' Hayley cried out. 'It might not be safe!'

Jude tugged Hayley back.

'Let her go,' she said. 'We're in the clear.'

Ebony hesitated and glanced back at Jude and Hayley. Hayley took a deep breath and resigned herself to the fact it was over, at least for them. She urged Ebony onwards.

'We'll meet you outside,' she said. 'Stay close.'

'I'll make sure she doesn't fall off the ledge,' Jude said. 'Wouldn't that be annoying, after all we've been through.'

'I'll join you in a minute,' Hayley said.

Jude bounded up the trail towards the cave mouth, guided by the light of Ebony's torch. Hayley watched her go and then rummaged in her backpack for the treat she had been saving. She retrieved her own torch and followed her wife and daughter out onto the plateau.

Ebony and Jude were craning their necks to observe the colony of bats as they disappeared into the night sky.

'They can fly hundreds of kilometres, you know,' Ebony said. 'They eat loads of insects.'

'We might have to start eating insects ourselves, the way things are going,' Jude said.

'In the meantime, we still have these,' Hayley said, as she approached from behind. 'Happy birthday, kiddo.'

She offered Ebony a packet of Twisties. Ebony's mouth fell open in shock.

'Can I?' she asked.

Hayley tore open the packet and plunged her hand inside. She pulled out a handful of chips and stuffed them into her mouth, eyelids flickering in pleasure. Jude snatched the bag of chips and shared them with Ebony. They enjoyed a moment of silent reverence, punctuated by the sound of satisfied crunching.

'So good,' Ebony said, gorging herself.

'*So* good,' Hayley agreed.

They ate without talking for a while, looking out over the state forest and listening to the sounds of the night. The sky was vast and cloudless, the moon a mere sliver. A galaxy of stars glimmered overhead. After a little searching, Ebony found the one she was looking for.

'That's Jupiter,' she told her mothers. 'See it?'

Hayley and Jude strained to make out the point of light amongst the splendour of distant suns.

'The star to the north is called Zubeneschamali,' Ebony said.

Hayley and Jude glanced at each other, impressed by their daughter's knowledge of astronomy.

'It's the only green one in the sky,' Ebony continued.

'That's beautiful, baby,' Hayley said, stroking Ebony's hair. Her daughter hummed with the electricity of life.

'Sky's not gone,' Ebony said, looking between her surprised parents. 'She's up there. She's stardust. We all are.'

ACKNOWLEDGEMENTS

THE OPENING SCENE OF THIS BOOK CAME TO ME IN A DREAM. I was amongst the families on the sidelines watching that footy game when the kids froze and began to sing. I had just got home from a tour of a hundred Australian bookstores, driving 7000 kilometres all by my lonesome. I was exhausted. The last thing I wanted was to start a new novel. But there it was, complete and undeniable. I wrote the first draft in a frenzy. The characters, the voices, the story, the horror – they tumbled out of me, clawing their way into life.

This happens to writers sometimes, and when it does, the safest course of action is to stay out of the story's way. The manuscript that resulted was probably an unholy mess, and I am forever indebted to the select few individuals who helped turn the dream (or more accurately the nightmare) into a readable reality. Undying thanks, then, to the following people: Brendan Fredericks, Vanessa Radnidge, Chrysoula Aiello, Rebecca Hamilton and Vanessa Lanaway. Each of you made this book a hundred times better. Or let's say nine times better, because that's much scarier.

Born in Belfast, Chris Flynn now lives in a small town in regional Victoria. He is the author of *Mammoth*, *The Glass Kingdom*, *A Tiger in Eden*, the story collection *Here Be Leviathans*, and three books for children in association with Museums Victoria, *Horridus and the Hidden Valley*, *Horridus and the Night Forest* and *The Quest for Kool*.

His work has appeared in *Spinning Around: The Kylie Playlist*, *Griffith Review*, *Kill Your Darlings*, *Monster Children*, *McSweeney's*, *The Paris Review*, *Meanjin*, *The Guardian*, *The Age*, *The Australian*, *The Big Issue*, *Australian Book Review* and many other publications.

Chris's books have been shortlisted for and won prizes such as the Indie Book Award, Commonwealth Book Prize, Russell Prize for Humour, Queensland Premier's Literary Award and Aurealis Award.

His mum and dad were foster parents. He grew up with more than 100 brothers and sisters, all aged under nine.

hachette
AUSTRALIA

If you would like to find out more about Hachette Australia, our authors, upcoming events and new releases, you can visit our website or our social media channels:

hachette.com.au

HachetteAustralia

HachetteAus